Lights were spinning
on the slopes above them,

... like dancing feet of the Devil. Raider emptied
his pistol at the ghostly apparition.

"You won't stop it like that," Doc cried.

"What the hell you want me to do?"

There was an explosive clap over the mine entrance. Jets of flame blasted up again. Smoke continued to flow out of the shaft. Raider pulled a
bandanna out of his back pocket and tied it over
his mouth.

Doc was gagging on the smoke. "Raider, we
had better turn back."

Raider picked up the torch and held it overhead
again. Doc could see the maniacal gleam in Raider's black eyes. The big man from Arkansas wasn't
scared anymore. He was angry.

THE GHOST MINE

BERKLEY BOOKS, NEW YORK

THE GHOST MINE

A Berkley Book/published by arrangement with
the author

PRINTING HISTORY
Berkley edition/October 1985

ISBN: 0-425-08190-7

A BERKLEY BOOK ® TM 757,375
Berkley Books are published by The Berkley Publishing Group,
200 Madison Avenue, New York, NY 10016.
The name "BERKLEY" and the stylized "B" with design
are trademarks belonging to Berkley Publishing Corporation.
PRINTED IN THE UNITED STATES OF AMERICA

Dedicated to
Mark and Spike

CHAPTER ONE

Doc Weatherbee's Studebaker wagon rattled through the cold Montana night, finding every pothole on the dusty trail that took them north. Raider sat next to Doc, not speaking, keeping his eyes trained ahead of them. Doc thought his partner's demeanor was as icy as the wind that blew around his head, chilling the few cells in his body that had resisted the gusts of Canadian air that swept down the line of the Rocky Mountains, delaying the arrival of spring. Doc shifted the reins into his left hand, using his right hand to fish for an Old Virginia cheroot in the pocket of his fine suit coat.

"You gonna fire up another one of them stink logs?" Raider asked through clenched teeth.

"It had crossed my mind," Doc replied, striking a sulphur match.

"That dad-blamed shit makes my guts want to—"

"Raider," Doc said, "before you launch off into one of your lengthy diatribes against cigar smoking, let me remind you that I did not protest when you shook me out of bed in the middle of the night. Nor have I complained once on this three-day chase."

"Yeah, Doc, but you know as well as I do that—"

"That we are pursuing a worthy cause," Doc chimed in. "Yes, I am aware of the situation and the nature of our duty. I only ask that you allow me to indulge in one of my few pleasurable vices."

"Aw, hell, I don't care if you smoke your fool brains out. Just keep this wagon movin'. Can't that danged mule go any faster?"

A puff of smoke disappeared into the wind as Doc shook Judith's reins. Judith twitched her ears and kept moving at a steady pace, seemingly undaunted by the conditions of the cold night. Raider hated traveling at such a slow gait, but he had little choice, as he had ridden his own mount into the ground in his effort to find Doc. The chestnut gelding had taken up lame right before he reached the widow's house in Idaho Falls. He probably wouldn't have been as worked up if they hadn't been chasing a man who had killed two Pinkertons.

Junior Bledman had escaped from Bill Demont and Levon Jerkins, the two men who had been assigned to take Bledman back to the territorial prison in Rock Springs, Wyoming. Bledman was due to hang for the murder of five sodbusters, from whom he had stolen thirty-five dollars in silver and a bay mare. Bledman was considered so dangerous that the territorial marshal's office would not send a deputy (or even two) to bring him back for the gallows. The territorial governor's office had hired the Pinkerton National Detective Agency for the task.

"We would've been the ones to bring him back if we hadn't been so slow on that case in Texas." Raider was coming down hard on himself.

"You can't think that way, Raider," Doc replied.

"Hell, Doc," Raider said, shifting on the wagon seat, "you know as well as I do that Demont and Jerkins weren't the men to take Bledman back to Rock Springs. I mean, you can't take nothin' away from them, but they were office boys, not tough like you and me."

"Yes, but you can't—"

"They never should have been given that duty. Hell, I don't know, I guess we all stand a chance to buy it, but Jerkins had a family and Demont was plannin' to get hitched soon. I feel responsible, Doc."

"Is that why you decided to go after Bledman without waiting for Allan Pinkerton to assign us to the case?" Doc challenged Raider's black eyes.

"How'd you find out about that?"

"I wired the home office yesterday, while you were sleeping."

"What'd they say?" Raider slumped, not sure if he was in trouble.

"To pursue the Bledman boys until we bring them back."

"Damn it, what'd I tell you! I knew they was more than one. Couldn't one man get the drop on Demont and Jerkins."

"Didn't you stay around Boise long enough to get all of the details?" Doc torched the end of the stogie, keeping the smoke away from his partner.

"No, I just heard that both of our men were killed and that Bledman had been spotted runnin' north, toward Canada. I wonder who's with him?"

"Our files stated that he has been known to travel with his two brothers, Ronnie and Lyle. Several years ago he also rode with a gang of his own making, but they either disbanded or were brought to justice."

"Hell, Doc, I liked old Jerkins, you know what I mean? didn't take to Demont so much, but he was all right. And just can't help thinkin' that you and me should have been assigned to bring back that varmint. And I also think it's up to us to make things right." There were anger and sincerity in Raider's tired voice.

"I wholeheartedly agree," Doc replied. "However, I do think that you should try to maintain an even temperment, Raider. You're not at your best when you allow your work to become clouded by emotion."

Raider reached down to grab the butt of his Colt .45 Peacemaker. He hoisted the weapon from his holster and spun the cylinder, making sure that all six shots were in place. Doc blew smoke into the breeze as Raider reholstered the pistol.

"Ain't nothin' gonna be clouded 'ceptin' Junior Bledman's neck on the end of a rope." Raider checked the bullets on his gunbelt.

"Yes, don't forget that we have to take him in, preferably alive."

"I wanna see the look on the face of the widow Jerkins when that trapdoor drops out and Junior Bledman's feet are swinging," Raider muttered. "As soon as we get to the next town, I'm gettin' me a fast horse. I suggest you do the same."

Doc urged Judith forward, keeping his eyes trained in the distance. For once, Doc missed the clean, warm sheets of his young widow. Raider had rousted him from a deep, dreamless sleep, forcing him to abandon the slender body that rested next to him. As the wind cut through him, Doc shrugged his shoulders, wondering when they would catch up to Junior Bledman. He hated the frigid darkness of the northland just as much as Raider. But he knew he would never be able to sleep until the Pinkerton killer was brought to justice.

Raider sat up and howled when they saw the dim light burning on the horizon. Doc's pocket watch said five o'clock, but there was still no dawn glow to the east. It would be a late sunrise. He wondered if Raider would let Judith get a couple of hours of sleep before they went on after Junior Bledman.

"Stop the damn wagon and give me a match." Raider snapped his fingers impatiently.

Doc pulled back the reins and, without question, fished a sulphur match from the pocket of his silk vest. Raider leapt from the wagon seat and struck the match against an old wooden sign that had been mounted on a rotted post. Doc read the sign in the circle of match light: COPPERHEAD, MONTANA, NUMBER THAT LIVE HERE UNKNOWN. Raider climbed back into the seat.

"Interesting," Doc said, scratching his chin.

"What?" Raider was peering toward the lone light in the distance.

"Our report on the Bledman brothers gives their home as Montana," Doc said. "Do you think they might have relatives hereabouts?"

"Shit, Doc, git that critter movin'!" Raider scowled and shook the reins.

"Slowly," Doc said. "We don't want to come up on anyone and surprise them. Not yet, at least."

Raider pulled his lever-action Winchester from under the wagon seat.

"If Bledman is in Copperhead, he's going to wish to God

he never met me." Raider had a strange smile on his lips.

Doc thought it best not to argue with a partner who was jacking a cartridge into the chamber of a Winchester. He urged Judith toward the light in the distance. Who, he wondered, would be awake at such an early hour? Even the hardest-working sodbuster did not rise until the sun had peeked over the eastern horizon with a half-opened eye.

Copperhead loomed out of the shadows, not much more than a few dilapidated structures. Doc halted the wagon and raised a hand to his lips, urging Raider to be silent as they moved. Both of them slipped quietly behind the building where the light burned. With his hand full of his .38 Diamondback, Doc ascended a set of wooden steps to steal a look into the confines of a cluttered storeroom. Through a knothole in the slapdash planked door, Doc saw a small, balding man at work, counting money.

"What is it, Doc?" Raider whispered, his hands gripping the Winchester.

"I'm not certain," Doc replied. "But I think we can forget the guns."

"I'm keeping this rifle on my hip." Raider turned his head, glancing in every shadowy direction.

The balding man looked up from his counting, as if he had heard their voices. He stood up and walked slowly toward the planked door. Doc thought he had better knock. The man halted when he heard the tapping.

"I got a gun!" the man cried. "Don't you come in here."

"He's got an iron," Raider said. "Doc, move out of the way."

"Sir," Doc called. "I'm sliding my credentials under the door. I'm a Pinkerton agent and I'm in pursuit of a fugitive from the law."

"Doc!" Raider cried. "You shouldn't oughta—"

The door swung open almost as soon as Doc had slipped his papers through.

"Hurry in," the balding man said, looking in both directions. When the man saw Raider, he shifted his wire spectacles on the end of his skinny nose.

"He's a Pinkerton too?" the man asked.

"Yes," Doc replied. "I know it's hard to believe, but he is

in the service of Allan Pinkerton. And might I inquire as to your name?"

"Roby," the man replied. "Leighton Roby. Git on in here, big man."

Raider clumped up the steps behind Doc. When they were inside, Roby quickly shut the door and pulled down the wooden latch. He stopped cold as he spun backward to face Raider's Winchester. Raider lowered the weapon.

"What are you scared of, mister?" Raider surveyed the room's shadows.

"I'm scared of losin' what little money I got left," Roby said. "My general store ain't seen a dime of profit since the minin' company left out of here. I was countin' my savin's when you two up and scared the bejesus out of me."

"Please accept our apologies." Doc removed his derby and bowed.

"No offense taken," Roby replied. "Y'all want a cup of hot coffee?"

"Look here," Raider said, "we come to—"

"Coffee would be fine." Doc glared sternly at his partner. Raider snorted like a buffalo. "Doc, we gotta—"

"Steady, Raider," Doc replied. "We can learn what we need to know without bullying this gentleman."

"Hope y'all like it black." Roby poured from a steaming pot on the stove.

They were in his storeroom, Doc thought. He probably had a bed up in the loft over the store. Most of the clutter in the storeroom was junk rather than merchandise. Roby apparently did not care about the state of his inventory.

"Sorry to hear that business is bad," Doc said, hoping to prompt Roby's tongue into bemoaning his misery. Sometimes a worried man would reveal much more than he intended.

"You don't know the half of it," Roby said. "I'm plannin' to clear out of here as soon as I can."

"Why's that?" Raider asked, lifting the steaming tin cup to his lips.

"Well, things got bad after the mining company left," Roby replied. "I didn't mind too much, though, because it was still knowed that Copperhead is the only town within a hundred miles in any direction. So I had stragglers, you know, drifters and prospectors, cowpokes, some trappers from Canada, and the occasional Injun. Oh yeah, big man, I done business with Injuns. I don't know where they get money, and I don't care. Course, they never would serve 'em over to the cantina—not while the sheriff was still around."

"What happened to the sheriff?" Raider's hand slipped down to his .45.

"He took off like the rest of the people that left with the miners," Roby replied. "That left just me and the cantina. Hell, I thought it was bad, but I didn't know what bad was until that fat son of a bitch come here. 'Scuse my French."

"We heard it before," Raider said. "What fat man?"

"Big bastard," Roby replied. "Rode in here two days ago. Told me he needed credit. Been takin' everything on credit."

"And there's no sheriff to stop him," Doc said.

Raider stood up and straightened his holster. "What's this boy call himself?"

"Said to call him J.B.," Roby replied. "I tried to get him to sign for the stuff he took, but he wouldn't."

"Junior Bledman." Raider scowled. "He's a fat sack of shit."

"Is he red-faced, with a scar across his cheek?" Doc asked.

"That's the man," Roby replied. "Is he the boy you're lookin' for?"

Raider leaned over in the storekeeper's face. "Where's this man holin' up?"

"He's been in the cantina across the street, has been for the last two nights, drinkin' an' carryin' on with a Mexican girl."

Raider slammed his fist into his hand. "Let's go, Doc."

"Easy," Doc replied. "Mr. Roby, is Bledman sleeping in the cantina?"

"No, he's been sleepin' in a shed out back of the old livery. The livery's closed down too."

"I'm ready to take him, Doc." Raider patted the stock of the Winchester.

"I agree that we must move. However, first we have to ascertain if it is indeed Junior Bledman in the cantina. When a positive identification is made, then we shall set about to apprehend him with all of our professional skills."

Roby laughed. "You talk like a goose-greased dandy."

"You should hear him after he's had a good night's sleep,"

Raider said. "You're right, Doc. Let's take this like we should. I want to follow . . . what do you call it?"

"Procedure," Doc replied, draining the coffee cup.

"Yeah, procedure," Raider grunted, his fingers turning white on the butt of the Winchester.

"Mr. Roby," Doc said. "May I impose upon you for another cup of this fine coffee?"

"You git rid of that ape that's been creditin' me and you can take any damned thing in the store," Roby replied. "Hell, if he leaves, I might just stay on here."

Roby poured another tin mug of coffee for Doc and then turned to Raider. The storekeeper's wide eyes were trained on the Winchester. He laughed nervously and shook his head.

"What's so funny?" Raider asked.

"I was just thinkin' that you look pretty mad," Roby replied.

"So?" Raider peered out from under the brim of his Stetson.

"Well," said the storekeeper. "I was just thankin' God that you ain't mad at me."

They moved onto the front porch of the general store with their hot cups of coffee in hand. A steel-blue glow emanated from behind a shadow-dusted ridge. Mr. Roby pointed toward the dried-mud beehive known as the Cantina de Lobo. One horse, an Appaloosa, had been tied to the single ring of a hitching post. Raider threw his coffee cup into the street.

"That's the horse that Jerkins was ridin'!" Raider pointed with the rifle.

Doc leaned over the rail of the porch, squinting. "Are you sure?"

"He always rode an Appaloosa," Raider replied. "I even tried to buy it off him once, when that bunch of us was assigned to guard that gold train in Mexico. Remember?"

"Still, we must be sure." Doc said.

"Cover me," Raider said. "I'm going to take a look."

"Raider . . ."

Before Doc could stop him, Raider was stomping across Copperhead's lone, muddy street. Doc removed the .38 Diamondback from his coat pocket and held it ready as Raider stalked through the mud to examine the Appaloosa.

"Kinda bullheaded, ain't he?" Roby asked meekly.

Doc was silent. He watched as Raider lifted up one of the flaps that covered the saddlebags. Roby adjusted his spectacles so he could take a better look.

"What'd this fellow do, Mr. Pinkerton?"

"Killed seven people—that we know of."

"Don't like the sound of that." He moved a little closer to the door.

Raider came back toward them, carrying one of the saddlebags in his left hand. He threw the saddlebag onto the porch. It landed at Doc's feet.

"His Pinkerton papers are in there—Levon Jerkins. The picture of his wife, too. In yonder's the man who killed Jerkins and Demont."

"Or someone who knows the man that killed them," Doc replied. "Bledman could have sold the mount to some unsuspecting drifter. I think we should wait until he comes out before we—"

"God in heaven," Roby said. "He's already out!"

Raider spun back toward the cantina. "Get inside, storekeeper. Now."

Doc peered over the rim of the tin cup toward the entrance of the cantina. A bulky shape filled the narrow doorway. Bledman staggered out into the street with cheap tequila dripping from his greasy beard. His head was bare, and a grimy duster covered his husky frame. When the morning glow hit his eyes, Bledman was blinded for a moment. Raider came off the porch with the Winchester cocked and ready. Doc dropped his coffee cup and raised his .38.

"Bledman!" Raider cried. "Stop it right there!"

Bledman shielded his eyes, squinting toward Raider.

"You got the wrong man," Bledman said.

"We're Pinkertons," Raider called. "We come to take you back to Rock Springs. And I think it'd be a good idea if you decided to come peaceable."

Bledman swayed like a drunken bear. He grunted and shook his shaggy head. Raider thumbed back the hammer on the rifle.

Doc sounded nervous. "Perhaps I'd better—"

The big man seemed dead calm. "Doc, I'm used to dealin' with scum like this. Let me handle it."

"How'd you find me?" Bledman growled.

"You make a wide trail," Raider replied. "Startin' with Demont and Jerkins. Keep your hands where I can see 'em."

Bledman laughed. "You sore cause I killed two of your
agents?"

Raider watched his hands. "I'm sore, boy. Just like the
widow that you made. We're all damned sore at you, Bledman.
And we're gonna take you back, one way or another. If you
come along quiet-like, there won't be any trouble."

"What if I don't want to go?" Bledman gaped at the rifle.

"Then you won't be around later to wish you had," Raider
replied.

Bledman's arms hung loosely at his side. If he was carrying
sidearms—and he almost certainly was—they would be hidden
inside his duster. Raider would have to take him immediately
if he moved. Bledman was damned quick for a big man. Bill
Demont had lost his throat to Bledman's quickness and a piece
of jagged metal.

"Aw hell, Pinkerton," Bledman said. "You an' me ain't got
no reason to kill each other. Why don't you just . . ."

Bledman whirled in a circle, causing his duster to fly up all
around his fat body. Raider fired the Winchester and sent a
slug through the empty shell of the duster. Doc hit the deck as
Bledman returned fire with a smaller pistol. Clods of mud
kicked up at Raider's feet.

Raider dived to his left, rolling through a half-dried mud
puddle and coming up with the Winchester's sight on Bledman's
chest. Bledman had emptied his pistol and was reaching for a
sawed-off scattergun in a fold of his duster. Raider squeezed
off another burst, catching Bledman squarely in the chest. The
fat man staggered forward, vomiting blood and raising the
scattergun in his left hand.

The Winchester barked again in Raider's hands. Bledman's
facial features disappeared under the barrage of lead. The fat
man fell forward onto the scattergun, tripping both triggers and
discharging two barrels of buckshot into his flabby abdomen.
His body quivered in a pool of red mud.

"You had to do it, didn't you?" Doc called from the porch.

"What was I supposed to do, just stand there and let him
kill me?" Raider had turned away from the body and would
not look back.

"No, but we could have taken a different course entirely. However, I suppose it doesn't do any good to belabor the point. I guess you want me to examine the body for you."

"Would you mind, Doc? You know how I hate blood and guts."

"I wish you hated them as much as you seem to enjoy spreading them," Doc groaned, rising to step off the porch.

As his partner bent over the body, Raider gazed to the south, wondering if Bledman's brothers were around. Maybe Junior hadn't seen them yet. Maybe he was planning a rendezvous with them later. As the north wind howled around them, Raider tried to be angry with himself for cheating the hangman. But when he thought about the crying widow of Levon Jerkins, he couldn't help but feel that he had gotten the job done by shooting Junior Bledman.

As Doc knelt over the body, Leighton Roby came back onto the front porch of the general store. Raider stood beside the storekeeper as his partner began to shift through Junior Bledman's bloodstained pockets. Roby was eyeing the body with unnatural interest.

"I wonder if he's carrying any money?" Roby wiped his sweaty forehead.

"Why do you care?" Raider's black eyes peered straight through the storekeeper.

"Boy, howdy," Roby said. "You took him fair and square, Mr. Pinkerton. I saw the whole thing through a keyhole."

"Then you write down what you saw," Raider barked. "Then you sign it. Don't lie, don't exaggerate. Just write it down."

"How come?" Roby's lower lip was trembling slightly.

"Because our boss likes to know when we kill somebody. He don't like bodies spread around unless it's legal-like."

"I'll do just that." He was already searching for a pencil in his pocket.

Doc stood up, holding a handful of Bledman's worldly possessions. Roby moved closer to gape at the carnage. Doc looked the storekeeper square in the eye. Roby wiped the sweat from his brow.

"Yes sir, I'm beholdin' to you fellas for sendin' him on to his reward," Roby said. "He was runnin' up quite an account bill. And I sure don't think he intended to pay me."

"Just what are you driving at?" Doc was growing tired of Roby's hints.

"Well, I was wondering if he had any gold or silver on him, Mr. Pinkerton. Maybe he could settle up with me now. I mean, with all respect due the dead, I'd appreciate it if . . ."

Doc unfolded his hand. "It just so happens that our unfortunate friend had several silver pieces on him. And if you could see fit to roll him in a blanket and tie up the body, you may indeed have these pieces of silver."

Roby hurried to his task. Raider stretched to work the tightness out of his shoulders. Doc stepped up on the porch and laid out the things he had found on Bledman's body.

"There isn't much left after a man dies," Doc said. "Especially the desperate sort of scoundrel that Bledman seemed to be."

"Anything interestin'?" Raider wondered if someone would look through his remains one day.

Doc shrugged. "The usual. A derringer, some small bullets, the money that Roby wants, a wanted poster, and . . . well, what is this?"

He held up a tattered piece of parchment. It had been handled by several dirty pairs of hands. A snaky pattern of six sets of parallel lines came together at a prominent "X" mark. The "X" had been circled.

"What do you make of it, Raider?"

"A map," the big man howled. "Three roads convergin' at one spot. Maybe . . ."

"Go on."

"Well, there's a spot south of here called Three Forks of the Sun," Raider said. "Three roads come together there at the Musselshell River."

"And why would Bledman have been interested in this spot?"

"Hell, I don't . . . Wait a minute, the stage! That's it. The stage runs there, goin' north and south. Maybe Junior and his brothers were plannin' to bushwhack the Wells Fargo coach."

"But why would Bledman have come here?"

"You heard old Roby there," Raider replied. "This is the only town in a hundred miles around these parts. Bledman had been locked up for a long time. Seems like he would want some whiskey and some . . . some of that good stuff. I could use some of that myself about now."

"And you think he planned to rendezvous with his brothers?"

"Doc, maybe I should—"

"He's all wrapped up," Roby called from the street. "What do you want me to do with him?"

"Tie him on his horse," Doc replied. "Across the saddle."

"No!" Raider cried.

Doc peered with disbelief at his partner. "I beg your pardon?"

"Look here, Doc," Raider offered. "If them boys is gonna hold up the overland stage, I think we oughta try and stop them. I'm thinkin' I should take the Appaloosa and ride to the Three Forks. You can follow me in the wagon after you throw Bledman there in the back of the—"

"Raider, I don't think you should go after the Bledmans by yourself," Doc said. "It's obvious that Junior Bledman saw his relatives before he landed here. If they're looking for him, as they no doubt will be, you might ride into a trap."

Raider picked up his Winchester.

"Say what you want, Doc, but I'm goin' to Three Forks on the Appaloosa."

He started for the mount that was tied across the muddy street.

"Raider, come back here."

Doc watched as the tall man from Arkansas jumped into the dead man's saddle. Raider turned the Appaloosa and guided it next to Doc. He pulled his Stetson down over his eyes.

"Don't worry, Doc," Raider said. "I won't try to take them alone. But if I can do anythin' to save that stage, I have to give it a shot. You follow me as soon as you can."

"You pig-headed Ozark ridge-running . . ." Doc was shaking his fist.

"I like you too, Doc. So long."

The Appaloosa's hooves kicked up clumps of dirt as Raider rode hard to the south. Doc shook his head and took out a cheroot. Roby was gawking at him.

"What you want me to do with that dead man?" Roby asked.

Doc let out an exasperated breath. "Put him in the wagon."

"About that silver?" Roby was rubbing his hands together.

"Here," Doc replied, tossing him the money. "Will that cover what he owed you?"

"And then some."

Roby pocketed the silver and started to drag the body across the street. Doc puffed on his cigar, watching as his partner moved out of sight. Raider was right to take off after the site on the crude map. Still, Doc couldn't help but feel that he should have waited until both of them were ready to go. Judith needed a rest. So did Doc. And surely, if anyone could single-handedly give the Bledman brothers a rough time, Raider was the perfect man for the task.

Raider rode hard to the south until the Appaloosa's coat was thick with lather. He slowed the animal when the plain rose into a series of bumpy hills. The Musselshell River flowed between the grassy knolls, winding parallel to the main road used by the stage. If the stage was coming south, Raider thought, it might be full of gold or copper from the northern mines of the Montana Territory. Coming north, it might be carrying payroll for the miners. Companies liked to pay in script. Raider rounded a bend in the river, wondering if he might find a spot to get the drop on the intersection at the main road. When he saw the yellow Concord coach on its side in the middle of the river, he cursed himself for being too late.

Water flowed over the dead team horses, which still rested in their harnesses. The driver and the shotgun rider had been killed. There had been no other passengers. Raider looked down in the water to see the two thick logs that rested on the river bottom. Both logs were weighted and set far enough apart to make an impassable barrier for the stage's wheels.

"I reckon Junior's brothers didn't feel like waitin'," Raider said.

Raider was wondering if he should wait for Doc. Doc would be damned slow with that mule. Raider spurred the Appaloosa and began to ride in circles, looking for the fresh patterns of hoofprints. There had been four horses in the bushwhackers' party. He followed the tracks upriver until they turned north. They were heading for the Canadian border. Raider spurred the Appaloosa across the springy grassland, following the tracks in the soft earth.

• • •

"Well, sir, he's all trussed up and ready to go to his happy hunting ground," said Leighton Roby.

Doc took off his pearl gray derby and wiped his forehead with his handkerchief. Roby had loaded the body like a sack of flour into the back of the wagon. The storekeeper was standing there rubbing his hands together. Doc replaced the derby on his head and reached into his pocket. He withdrew the tattered map and gave it to Roby.

"Are you familiar with the area known as Three Forks of the Sun?" Doc had not been able to locate the area on his own map of the region.

"Sure do, Mr. Pinkerton. Just two hours' ride south of here. That where your partner was headed?"

"Yes," Doc replied. "And judging by the alacrity with which he rode out of here, I'd say he'll reach there in less than two hours."

Roby laughed and peered to the south. "Seems he's the kinda boy that does somethin' once he sets his mind to it."

"Stubborn is the word."

He left the porch of the general store and walked over to his wagon. Judith swayed in her harness, asleep on her feet. Doc had to give her a rest. He slipped the feed bag over her ears so that she would be able to eat when she woke up. He went back to the porch where Roby still stood.

"Is there any place hereabouts where I might purchase another mount?" Doc asked. "My mule is simply too tired to go another foot."

Roby shook his head. "Like I done told you, the livery's closed down and me and the cantina is the only ones left. Hell, there ain't a horse to be begged, borrowed, or stole in this town."

Doc looked to the south. He would have to wait while Judith rested. Raider was on his own for a while. Doc sat down in a chair on the porch of the general store. He propped up his legs and leaned back, drifting off into a fitful slumber. He dreamed that Raider was trapped by the Bledmans, who were intent on killing him. A rough hand stirred him from his reverie.

"Wake up, Mr. Pinkerton."

Doc opened his eyes and gasped for breath.

"You was hollerin' somethin' awful," Roby said. "Was you havin' a nightmare or somethin'?"

"How long was I out?" Doc stood up, trying to get his bearings.

"Been about three hours."

Judith brayed, shaking her head, trying to dislodge the feed bag. Doc jumped to his feet and accommodated her, allowing her to drink from a murky horse trough. When she had drank, she stomped her foot in the mud, as if she knew Doc was ready to go.

"Good luck, Mr. Pinkerton," Roby called as Doc hopped into the wagon seat.

Doc shook the reins, urging Judith south. The Studebaker rattled away from Copperhead, leaving the storekeeper to mind the affairs of the one-horse town. When Doc was well along the way, he reached into his pocket to check his .38 Diamondback. He hadn't liked the idea of leaving Raider alone for so long, even if his choice had been dictated by physical circumstance.

"Judith," he said, "would you mind walking a bit faster."

He reached the Musselshell River just after midday. The sun was warming the cool air, stirring up the buzzards that rode the air currents overhead. Doc climbed down and examined the area, noting the fresh tracks of five horses, one of which had to be Raider's Appaloosa. He glanced back toward the overturned Concord coach. A vulture had landed on the seat and was beginning to peck at the eyes of the dead driver, who was still strapped into his post.

The right thing to do was bury the driver and the shotgun rider. Doc cursed Raider for leaving him to the task by himself. He removed his coat and his Melton overgaiters, and then waded into the cold stream with his pants rolled up to his thighs. When he had untied the driver, he looked around for the body of the shotgun driver, which was lodged downstream between two boulders. Doc dragged the driver's body to shore and then retrieved the body of the shotgun rider. As he came back along the riverbank he noticed that a buzzard was circling his wagon. The body of Junior Bledman was starting to ripen in the warm air.

The smell hit Doc's nose when he opened the back of the wagon. He reached in for a small spade, which had been covered by Bledman's body. He rolled out the package that had been wrapped up by Leighton Roby. When he finally found the spade, he decided to bury Junior Bledman as well. There was no need to cart the corpse all over creation. Doc would mention the place and reason for the burial in his report. If he was going to chase after Raider, he didn't need any dead men along to hinder him.

"I wish I could have the sense of humor possessed by Hamlet's gravedigger," Doc said to himself.

He started to think ill of Raider for leaving him to the arduous task, but he remembered several times that Raider had been left to clear up the mess. Doc dragged all three bodies to some soft earth by the streambed. He would use river rocks as tombstones and to keep out scavengers that might unearth the bodies.

He laid the driver in the first shallow grave, throwing thick, rich earth over the faded skin. The shotgun driver went in the next hole, followed by Junior Bledman in the third trench. Doc broke a sweat as he heaped rocks on the first two graves. When he looked at Junior Bledman's grave, he decided to forgo the stones. He didn't want to waste any more time before he started after Raider. Besides, he thought, Bledman didn't deserve a marked resting place. And as far as Doc was concerned, the coyotes and vultures could pick the body until clean, white bones were bleached dry by the yellow sun.

CHAPTER TWO

As near as Raider could figure, the Bledman boys were heading toward the sloping woodlands near the Canadian border. He had ridden fast until dark, keeping one eye over his shoulder to look back for Doc. He thought about backtracking to find his partner and then pick up the trail again. But the Bledmans were moving fast, and once they reached the woods, they might hole up anywhere and he would never find them. At dusk, Raider slowed the Appaloosa and fixed himself on the North Star. He would plod through the darkness and chase them for one more day. After that, they would be into the forests and then probably gone for good. At least he had taken Junior Bledman, to make up for Demont and Jerkins.

Raider nodded in the saddle, leaning forward to catch several tossed hours of sleep. Just before dawn, he awoke with his boots still in the stirrups to find the Appaloosa sleeping. He wondered how long they had been in that same spot. Raider urged the Appaloosa toward the red shadows on the sunrise horizon.

By noon, the blue treetops of the low-lying forests were looming in front of him. The forest floor would not give up tracks so easily. Raider reached the treeline two hours after he saw the mountain ahead of him. He dismounted and walked the Appaloosa along the smooth rocks of a dried riverbed that ran back into the sloping trees. Raider scrutinized every scratch on every rock, broken twigs, crushed lichens, and soapweed tufts. The area had been well traveled. Horseshoes had sparked splinters of rock and gravel. The signs indicated a route to the west, along the treeline. Raider silently thanked Lone Eagle, the Shoshone scout who had taught him how to track.

Raider looked back to the south, watching for Doc again. He wondered if Doc would quit following him. But then, he thought, Doc had never quit on anything in his whole life. He'd be cussing and moaning, but he'd keep coming. Raider jumped into his saddle and started west, following the dried riverbed.

Dark clouds rolled over the forests as Raider plodded into the thick forest. Having trees all around him didn't make him feel any safer. Four men with repeating rifles could fire a lot of slugs from between the tree trunks. And one of them was bound to hit his mark. Raider removed his Winchester from the saddle scabbard. He jacked a round into the chamber and spurred the Appaloosa forward. He planned to be a loaded, moving target.

Light rain fell, bringing an early dusk. Raider continued blindly through the dismal wilderness, driven on by his sense of duty. The riverbed had disappeared completely, leaving only a narrow path through the trees. Raider endured the rain until he saw the blurred circle of light in the distance. He had come as far as he could. He would stop for a while and then turn back. Like Doc always said, they could file a report later.

Bolts of lightning crashed over the treetops as Raider tied the Appaloosa to the hitching post outside the dilapidated wooden structure that housed the dim light. The place was too far off the main trails to be anything but an old trapper's outpost that had somehow survived on new business from prospectors and timber crews. The rickety steps sagged under his weight. He knocked soundly on the wood-planked door. A small man in buckskins met him at the threshold.

"Get on in out of the rain, cowboy. Name's Henry. Boy, howdy, your Stetson's really drippin'. How 'bout a cup of hot coffee? Only five cents."

Raider's hand rested on the butt of his Peacemaker. He stepped into the shack, holding the Winchester under his left arm. Two miner's lamps illuminated the dusty enclosure. Raider guessed that Henry was selling supplies for grubstakes to the silver and gold country. Stacked around the walls were bags of beans, salt, coffee, lard, and meal. Picks and shovels hung over a knotty counter. In the other half of the store, under one of the miner's lamps, three men were huddled around a table, playing poker. Raider took a long look at them.

"Just a friendly game, cowboy," Henry said. "You want coffee?"

Raider's hand was on his pistol as he spoke loudly enough for all of them to hear.

"Four men robbed a stage down south of here. They mighta come this way, loaded with money. Probably lookin' for supplies."

Henry glanced at the table where the men were playing poker. Two of the men stood up and backed away from the table. They were dressed in buckskins like Henry. The third man was wearing a gray sombrero and a slicker like the one on Junior Bledman. Raider drew his Colt and thumbed back the hammer.

"You ridin' with the Bledmans?" Raider asked the man in the slicker.

"Don't know 'em." The man did not show fear or anger.

"He rode in here with three other boys," Henry said. "They left when he stayed to play poker. Gave me twenty dollars in script and gold for supplies. Bought six boxes of ammo—"

A quick burst of temper from the slicker man: "Shut up, old man."

Raider couldn't see his face under the shadows of the wide-brimmed sombrero. The man just sat there. His manner turned cold and calm again.

"I ain't done nothin'," he said to Raider. "I earned that money prospectin' with my brothers."

"If that's true, then you don't have nothin' to worry about." He waved the Colt. "Now put your hands up on the table where I can see 'em."

A serpent's tongue of fire erupted from under the man's slicker. A slug slammed into the wooden plank above Raider's head. Raider squeezed the trigger of the Colt, piercing a second hole in the slicker. The man at the table slammed back against the wall and then fell forward with the rebound, thudding into the pile of wagered money. Blood pooled underneath him. The three men in buckskins came up off the floor as the smoke started to clear. Henry put a finger into his ear.

"Kinda sets your head to ringin', don't it?"

"I'll take that coffee now," Raider said. "Unless you boys are with that dead man."

"No sir," Henry said. "We're just honest men around here."

Raider tried to avert his eyes from the body. "Tell me about the boys that this one was ridin' with."

Henry grimaced. "They was ugly and nasty. I was glad they didn't rob me. They rode out when that other boy decided to stay and play cards."

"You sure you ain't with them?" Raider stared him down.

Henry laughed. "Hell, stranger, I had this place since the first gold rush in forty-nine. Ever' time I git a notion to close down, another fool prospector comes along and buys a dollar's worth of beans."

"What about them two?" Raider asked, pointing at the other pair of trembling mountain men.

"Jeremiah and Zeb," Henry replied. "They trap some and pack sundries in for me. Do the best they can."

Raider looked toward the corpse. He didn't see any sense in taking the dead man with him. He still had to look for the other three men in the rain. Henry handed him a full cup of coffee.

Raider leaned back against the counter. "Did his buddies say anything to this one about meetin' later?"

"Said they was goin' back to camp," Henry replied.

Raider's body snapped to attention. "If they're close by, maybe I can catch 'em off guard."

"Won't do much good in this storm," Henry said.

"Keep the lamp burnin' for me." Raider pulled up his collar.

"What about all that silver on the poker table?"

"Bury the body and it's yours."

Henry clapped him on the back. "I'm startin' to like you, stranger."

Raider opened the door and stepped out into the rain. The

sky was dark and clouded. Occasional bursts of spectral light illuminated the silhouetted branches of the ponderosa pine trees. Raider could barely see two feet in front of his face. Following or searching for the rest of the Bledman gang would be impossible with these sheets of water hindering him. He would have to wait until the rain let up.

As he turned back toward the steps, a streak of lightning revealed three dark figures rushing headlong from the shadows. He reached for his Colt, but a rap on his shoulder kept him from finding the gun butt. Raider felt his gun hand go numb. A second blow caught him at the base of the neck, rendering him immobile and sending him face-first into a deep, murky puddle of mud.

When Raider stirred from unconsciousness, his black eyes opened to flickers of orange torchlight on rock walls. He was lying on dry, solid ground. Sharp pain seemed to encompass his entire body. Water was trickling somewhere, with echoed rumblings of thunder in the background. Three voices came behind the echo.

"Them trappers didn't have much," said a high voice. "We shoulda killed them."

"Naw," replied a deeper voice. "If we kill 'em, we won't be able to rob 'em again in a couple of months. We got a month's supplies, too."

"But they helped that Pinkerton kill Jimmy," said a third voice.

"Jimmy weren't our kin, Lyle."

"I bet he killed Junior."

"I ain't your kin either," said the third voice. "Y'all gonna forget about me when we get in a rough spot?"

"Don't talk like that to Ronnie!"

"Both of you shut up!" boomed the leader—Ronnie Bledman, Raider guessed. "Jake, you check on the Pinkerton over there."

The toe of a boot kicked Raider in the side. He rolled over, only to realize that his hands were tied. He looked up at a weasel-faced man in a floppy felt hat. Raider knew that his holster was empty. Had they found the hunting knife in his boot? The pressure was there against his leg.

"He's awake," said the weasel.

"Don't look like much to me," said the high voice of Lyle Bledman.

"Be careful," replied Ronnie. "Them Pinkertons can be a mite ornery if you don't watch 'em careful-like."

The three figures came into focus for Raider. Ronnie was the big man in a ratty Confederate officer's coat and hat. Lyle wore a slicker and a black derby with a feather in it. Jake, the weasel, held a Wells Fargo pocket revolver on Raider.

"Let me kill him, Ronnie," Jake howled. "He's got to learn that he can't mess around with the Bledmans. Let me kill him, Ronnie, I'll show you that I'm as good as kin."

Ronnie Bledman's eyes were burning. Raider looked up into the twin barrels of a Remington scattergun. Even if Raider could get to the knife in his boot, it wouldn't have made much difference against a pistol and a shotgun. Ronnie Bledman thumbed back both hammers of the scattergun.

"Stand up, Pinkerton."

Raider tried to move but found that his joints were stiff. Jake prodded him with a boot. Raider tried again, but he could not maintain his balance.

"I can't stand up until you untie my hands."

"You think I'm stupid enough to fall for somethin' like that?" Ronnie Bledman said. "I ain't cuttin' that rope."

"There's three of you," Raider replied. "Aw hell, if you ain't gonna untie me, then lift me up."

Lyle and Jake lifted Raider to his feet. Ronnie Bledman stepped closer to him. His face was scarred and unshaven. His crooked nose had been broken several times. Raider forced a confident smile.

"You kill my boy Jimmy?" Ronnie Bledman asked.

"He shot at me first."

"How about Junior? What happened to him? Why didn't he meet us at Three Forks?" Lyle Bledman was raving like a madman.

Raider stayed cool. "Hell, Junior lost us. That brother of your'n can outrun anybody."

"I guess so," Bledman replied. "So he should be showin'

up here pretty soon. Shouldn't he?"

Raider shrugged. "I guess so."

Ronnie rubbed his grizzled chin.

"What if you're lyin' to me, Pinkerton?"

"Why would I be lyin'? You think I'm proud that he got away from me?"

"He's lyin'," Jake cried. "And he ain't alone, neither. Them Pinkertons never travel by theirselves."

"Junior killed my partner," Raider replied.

"What kind of gun he get him with?" Ronnie asked quickly.

"Sawed-off scattergun," Raider shot back.

Ronnie Bledman swung the butt of the shotgun into Raider's stomach. Raider buckled to his knees. He grabbed Bledman's legs and drove him quickly into a rocky wall of sandstone. He came up with his tied fists, hammering Bledman's chin. As Bledman slumped to the ground, Raider dropped his hand down to his boot, bringing up the hunting knife and spinning it in the air to lodge in the throat of the man named Jake. The shotgun butt cracked into his back again, sending him to the ground.

"Shoot him, Ronnie!" Lyle Bledman cried.

"Shut up, brother." Ronnie scowled. "Git me my bag. I'm gonna make this bluebelly sorry that he done that to me."

"I ain't a bluebelly!" Raider cried. "I'm the pride of Dixie, boy."

Bledman pressed the muzzle of the shotgun against Raider's temple. "Stand up, Pinkerton!"

As Raider stood, he was aware for the first time that they were inside a torchlit cave. The trickling sound of water was the waterfall at the entrance to the cave. Bledman was probably holding up in a place called Eagle Falls, way up in the forest of the high country. They were right on the border of Canada and the Montana Territory, in the lower ranges of the Rockies. An army of men might not be able to find Bledman in the forests. Indians didn't even come near Eagle Falls. It was bad medicine.

"You're mighty big with a hand cannon and your brother backin' you up," Raider said. "What's the matter, Ronnie? Can't stand a fair fight?"

u'll allow me to reach into my coat pocket."
 nodded. "Go ahead. But I see a flash of steel, you'll
 ' air through a hole in your chest."
oved slowly as he retrieved his credentials from his
at pocket. He held the paper up for Henry to see. He
, but the buckskinned man wouldn't take it from his

partner, I can't even read. Looks like I'm either going
 shoot you or take your word for it. What'll it be?"
y honor as a Pinkerton and a gentleman, I will not
." Doc waited patiently for Henry to decide.
ckskinned trader lowered his rifle. "Good enough."
 can you tell me where I might find my partner?"
 the forest, I reckon." He pointed up into the moun-
em boys you called Bledman robbed me last night
 your partner with them. They camped up high, I
aybe near the falls."
ou take me there?"
shook his head. "Ain't no need for me to risk my
 I don't want to tangle with the Bledman boys again.
y they didn't kill us."
dded, sizing up the high-country trader. He was a
 didn't have much. A man who might be interested
back what had been taken from him. It was worth a
hought.
lp you recover your property, will you take me into
ountry?" Doc raised an eyebrow and tempted him
le.
licked his lips. "You gettin' me with that one. But
now you can get back what they took?"
sed his right hand. "I *am* a Pinkerton above all. If
 do it, then I can."
 mister, you talk a blue streak."
e Weatherbee." He extended his hand to the trader.
ighed. "Hell, Weatherbee, let's go. If I don't git
oney, I'm gonna be dead soon anyway."
t out for another path that began at the timberline.
slow and deliberate as he cut through the trees. Doc
 steps, leading Judith behind him. It was almost
before Doc heard the water trickling down the slope.

Again Bledman hit him in the stomach. Raider stumbled
backward but did not go down. Lyle Bledman came up next
to his brother.

"I ain't afraid of nothin', Pinkerton," Bledman cried. "And
I ain't afraid to take what I want. Ain't a sin for a man to
survive himself."

Raider spat blood. "Is killin' a sin? Or stagecoach robbin'?"

"Blow his head off, Ronnie!" Lyle cried.

"Shut up, Lyle!"

Raider wanted to stir them up. "Go on, shoot me down in
cold blood. You ain't got the guts to face me man to man."

Ronnie Bledman pushed Raider against a cave wall. Raider's
legs were wobbly, but he could still stand. Bledman gave the
shotgun to his little brother. Lyle handed him a leather bag.
Bledman smiled through tobacco-stained teeth.

"You gonna git what you got comin' to you, Pinkerton.
Lyle, make him turn his belly to the wall."

Raider kept after Ronnie. "Turn me around so your brother
can shoot me in the back. I'd clean you in a fair fight, you
bastard."

Bledman reached into the leather bag and unrolled a short
buggy whip. A strand of knotted copper wire was attached to
the end of the lash. Bledman stepped forward and ripped away
the back of Raider's shirt.

"I reckon I ought to save you for Junior," Ronnie said. "But
I think it's up to me to teach you a lesson, Pinkerton."

Bledman slapped the wire lash against the wall. Raider
gritted his teeth. The knotted copper struck dangerously close
to his ear. Raider tensed, waiting for the sting.

Lyle Bledman danced a madman's jig. "He's dreadin' it.
You gonna make a coward out of him. Look at him, Ronnie."

"You gonna learn the hard way," Bledman snarled. "This
one's comin' right in the thick of your hide."

Bledman laid the copper lash in the middle of Raider's back.
Raider flinched, but he didn't cry out. The second strike cut
into his skin. Raider didn't utter a single noise.

"He's got guts for a Pink boy," Lyle said. "Hit him again,
Ronnie. Hit him hard."

Ronnie licked his cracked lips. "He's gonna hurt. I'm gonna

make him beg for mercy on his knees."

As he drew back the whip, Raider felt a surge of strength rushing through his body. When the lash stung him, he wheeled on the balls of his feet, charging headlong into Lyle Bledman. The shotgun went off with a deafening clap, sending a load of buckshot into the cave roof. Lyle tumbled backward as his brother fumbled for a pistol inside his coat.

"Kill him, damn it!" Ronnie cried.

Raider staggered for the front of the cave, working his hands loose. Water fell over the opening. Raider couldn't see a path as he looked out into the darkness. There was no way to tell how high the falls were. He turned back to see Ronnie Bledman aiming a Navy Colt at his chest. Raider took a step into the night as the Colt exploded. Momentarily, he felt the cold water hitting the whip marks on his back. Then he fell backward, tumbling off the waterfall, into the wet circle of darkness below.

Doc Weatherbee took the wagon as far as it would go up the dried, rock-paved riverbed. When he saw the path leading into the trees, he unharnessed Judith and then locked the wagon's compartment, draping a sign over the side that read: *This wagon used to carry Indians with smallpox. Touch at your own risk.* Usually the sign was enough to ward off any curious drifters who might do damage with clumsy hands.

"Leave it to Raider to get lost on the backside of Hell," Doc groaned as he led Judith between the trees.

The forest was alive with early morning activity. Doc had followed the trail through the night, lolling half-conscious in the seat while Judith trudged into the wilderness. So far there had been none of Raider's usual carnage along the way—dead bodies, wounded men, and the occasional deceased horse. Doc hoped he would catch up to his partner before he found the Bledman gang. It would be a lot easier to keep everyone alive that way.

A whitetail buck shot across the path, scaring Doc out of his musings. His hand was gripped tightly on the handle of his .38 Diamondback. He had a few surprises in the saddlebag on Judith's back. If only he lived to use them. He continued on the narrow trail toward an open area ahead of him, beyond the

thick woodland. The wooden structure
in the sheen of morning light. Doc
the dwelling.

As he tied Judith's reins to the hit
sound of a Winchester's lever behi
toward the sound, he saw the smal
smiled and tipped his hat. He alw
cordial when someone got the drop

"Good day, sir, Weatherbee's the
to—"

"Keep your hands where I can s
buckskins.

"Who is it, Henry?" asked a voi
"Don't know," Henry replied. "B
You hold up your hands and come slo
Doc obeyed the rifle. "I assure
mean no harm to you or your friends
in this area and I—"

"I done had me enough of bu
replied. "Dad-blamed bunch of sid
take ever'thing. Too much civiliza
ain't got a chance to be God-feari

"Yes," Doc said, lowering his ha
Mr. Henry, I'm looking for my p
him hereabouts."

"Partner? What's he look like?
"A rather tall fellow. Black hai
the shoulders. Rough. Crude."
"Sounds like that marshal wh
for those stagecoach robbers. Kil
Doc sighed and nodded. "Th
enjoys that sort of thing. Have y
"Not so fast," Henry said.
partner? Are you a marshal too?
"We're Pinkerton operatives,
We're on the trail of the Bledm
"Pinkertons, huh," Henry sai
on Doc. "That makes sense. Yo
Pinkerton?"

He asked Henry to take him to the falls.

"Might get us a handful of bushwhackers," Henry said.

Doc withdrew the .38 Diamondback from his pocket. "Then we will shoot them." He meant it.

Henry turned around and pushed through the brush toward the sounds of running water. The pool at the base of the falls was not wide, but it was deep. Doc knelt to scoop a handful of crystal liquid to his lips. Judith bent to drink, as did Henry. When Doc's thirst was quenched, he looked up the slope to the top of the falls.

"Sometimes a cave is hidden behind the water," Doc said. "Are you aware of such a place, Mr. Henry?"

"Not rightly." Henry's eyes were darting nervously in all directions.

"Perhaps I should have a look down here." Doc rose. "Keep me covered as I walk around the pool."

"Hey, I thought you was gonna git my stuff back."

"Patience, Henry," Doc replied. "After all, you have procured my services for nothing."

"I git killed and it won't be for nothin'." Henry slid cautiously back into the brush with his rifle cocked.

Doc slipped around the pool, keeping his eyes up to watch the forest. When he neared the falling stream, he peered into the dull, translucent wall of water. The vague hue of human skin was apparent on the other side of the fall. Doc removed his coat and his footwear and dived headlong into the icy pool. Henry ran toward the fall when he saw Doc go into the drink. He thought the dandy had gone crazy until he saw him swimming back with Raider's body tucked under his arm.

Raider knew he was alive because the pain was so great in every bone and muscle of his body. He sensed motion and heard a familiar tone of voice. When the voice became clearer, Raider thought he might be dead and in Heaven, and that Doc was there to bother him. But he felt the pressure and warmth of several blankets to reassure the continuation of his aching life.

"His fever's broken," Doc said, holding a hand on Raider's forehead.

Raider knocked Doc's hand away. "You ain't my momma."

"Good, he's surly," Doc said. "Here, drink this."

When Raider's eyes focused, he realized he was inside Henry's shack. Doc was holding out a bottle to him. Raider took it and drank, thinking the bottle held whiskey. Instead, he swallowed a sweet, honey-tasting liquid.

"What the hell is this?" Raider wiped his mustache.

"Indian medicine," said Henry, who stood behind Doc. "Best be glad we found you. Your partner's doctorin' done saved your life."

Raider felt a churning in his belly, like he had to puke his guts out. He threw back the blankets and ran for the door. Henry shrugged as Raider decorated his front steps.

"Does that to you sometimes," the trader chortled.

"A cathartic effect," Doc rejoined.

Raider turned back toward them, wiping his mouth. He took a few steps and stopped. Quickly he spun back toward the door and made a run for the outhouse.

Henry laughed again. "Does that sometimes too!"

"We shouldn't be laughing at him," Doc said. "Oh well, at least he's up and around."

Raider came back in ten minutes, buttoning his pants. "Almost didn't make it," he groaned.

"How are you feeling?" Doc asked.

Raider held his head. "I'm sore. Damn! I think that Injun beer did me some good. I ain't as dizzy as I was when I woke up."

"Drainin' the old flooder didn't hurt none either!" Henry added.

"I guess I'm beholdin' to you both." His thanks were awkward.

"Your partner's the one come after you," Henry replied.

"Do you remember anything, Raider?"

"Just dreams, Doc, and none of them too clear. I know I came pretty close to catchin' Ronnie and Lyle Bledman. Doc, I'm feelin' good enough to go back up there and look for them."

"A tribute to your iron constitution," Doc said. "But I'm afraid we'll be outmanned if we go up there. You were out for two days, and during that time a few changes have occurred."

Raider glared at them. "Changes? What kind of changes?"

"Some of Bledman's kinfolk been passin' through," Henry replied. "'Bout thirteen of 'em up there, near as I counted. Had to hide you and your buddy back here. At least none of 'em tried to rob me."

Raider slumped over with his head in his hands. "Doc, you got any ideas of why they're bunchin' up there?"

Doc shrugged. "It could be anything. A train job, a payroll. Maybe they plan to avenge Junior's death. These people can be very clannish."

"I guess there's nothing we can do, then," Raider groaned.

"I didn't say that," Doc replied. "I simply remarked that we couldn't ride up there and go head to head with them."

Raider leaned back and glared at Doc. "You was thinkin' while I was sleepin'. What you got up your sleeve?"

Doc looked at the mountains. "Given the cramped nature of the high-country terrain, we might well exploit a tight fit to entrap the Bledmans. All of them, at that."

"What's that mean to them of us ain't had no book learnin'?" Henry asked.

"I think he means that we've got to get the Bledmans in a ravine or in the forest, where we can get the drop on them," Raider said. "Only we got to have a special kinda place."

"You're absolutely on target, Rade. Mr. Henry, do you know of such a place? It would have to be on the direct route that the Bledmans would take down to get out of the high forest."

Henry studied them with dubious eyes. "You two serious about this?"

Doc nodded. "Most assuredly."

"Hell," Henry laughed. "I guess you are. Now, let me think on it. If they up high, they gonna have to ride down through the pass, up by Blackfoot Holler. That's the only way to get over the mountain, to the higher rangers, so if they went up that way, they have to come back the same route."

"How narrow is this pass?" Doc asked.

"Only big enough for two men to walk abreast, or one horse."

"And you're sure they'll come down that way?" Raider asked skeptically.

"It's the quickest path."

"Do you have an ax, Mr. Henry?" Doc asked.

"Sure," Henry replied. "What for?"

Doc looked at Raider.

"Oh no," Raider said. "You ain't givin' me another one of them chicken-pluckin' jobs, Doc. You always—"

"Do you want to catch the Bledmans?" Doc asked.

"Aw, hell, Doc. I'm still sore all over."

"Chopping wood will help you work out the kinks," Doc replied. "It's the only way, Raider. Take it or leave it."

"Dad-blamed chicken-pickin' jobs!"

Doc was glad to see that his partner was angry. It meant that Raider was going to live. Anger also gave him a hell of a lot of energy.

Doc had been right again. Swinging the ax had helped the soreness in Raider's body. He broke a sweat felling four fat-man-thick pines, stripping their branches, and staking them at each end of the pass, one on each side. They stacked rocks and small boulders on the length of all four logs, heaping up a narrow wall of stone. When the rocks were in place, Doc produced four sticks of dynamite. He capped them and then worked the red lengths down into all four walls of stone. The ravine was so narrow that they crossed back and forth on a single wooden plank.

"Listen," Henry said as Doc put the last stick in place. "Comin' down the trail."

"Think they heard us choppin' wood?" Raider searched for movement in the trees.

"It doesn't matter now," Doc replied. "Both of you get into place. On my command, use your rifles to detonate the charges. Make sure you hide behind the foliage."

"What'd he say?" Henry asked.

"Get back in the trees and blast those dynamite caps when he gives the word," Raider replied. "And make sure you're not too close to that dynamite. Understood?"

"I hope this works," Henry said. Then he added with a laugh, "Damn me if I ain't excited for the first time in twenty years!"

Everyone slipped back to their respective posts. Doc extended his spyglass, peering toward each makeshift wall of rock. He planned to catch the Bledmans in midstream with an impromptu slide of stone. Once he had them, he hoped he would be able to deliver the final blow. He spied a dark felt hat bobbing between the trees.

"It won't be long," he called to Raider and Henry.

Doc counted thirteen of them on the path, just as Henry had said. Lyle Bledman was leading the way, with his big brother riding second. All of them would never fit into the ravine. Doc would still have to give it a try.

They had to walk their horses through the narrow pass. Doc waited until Lyle and Ronnie were inside the ravine. Four more of the clan trickled in behind them before Doc shouted to Henry and Raider. "Now!" he bellowed.

Raider's rifle exploded first. The rocks tumbled down in front of them. A boulder caught Lyle Bledman's head and knocked him to the ground. Raider fired the second shot to bring down the other half of the avalanche. When Henry was slow on the back section, Raider fired two more times, helping him along. The other two logs rolled down, trapping the six riders and cutting off the back seven from the rest of the party.

When the smoke started to settle, Doc cried out again. "Bledman!" he called. "You're trapped. Give it up. I've got thirty Pinkerton agents surrounding you."

The captive party below them answered with gunfire. Doc could see the free members starting to spread out. They might never survive a firefight in the woods. Doc shoved a fuse into another stick of dynamite and torched it. He stood up and threw the charge in the general direction of the free Bledmans. He hit the ground just as the explosion shook the forest.

Doc called again through the smoke. "You can't escape. And unless your men surrender right away, I'm going to toss a hot potato into the pass. Say goodbye to your kin."

Doc waited for a minute to let them talk it out. Raider was sitting back in the trees, wondering if Doc would really blow up all those men. It wasn't like him to kill so recklessly. Maybe it was their only chance.

"I'm lighting the fuse, Ronnie," Doc persisted. "Do you hear it?"

The fizzling of the fuse was the most audible sound in the quiet forest. Even the Bledmans were silent below.

Doc's voice pierced the air. "Do or die!" he called. "What are you going to do, Bledman? You've got three seconds to decide."

"Don't!" cried Ronnie Bledman.

"Tell your men to give themselves up!"

"Do it," Bledman shouted. "Come on, hurry!"

Doc extinguished the fuse, which was not attached to anything but his hand. Raider and Henry moved toward him as Bledman's men came out of the trees with their hands over their heads. Raider held his rifle on them while Henry tied them up.

"We got all seven of them," Raider said. "How we gonna git the other six out of that hole?"

"Come with me," Doc started off through the trees.

Raider thought Doc was damned smart and tough for the way he got Ronnie Bledman to surrender. First he stood behind a tree holding a stick of red thunder in his hands. He held a lit cheroot close to the fuse and then urged the Bledmans to drop all their guns at one end of the ravine. Then he ordered Ronnie Bledman to tie the other four men belly down on their saddles. But not Lyle Bledman—he had been killed by the falling boulder, so he remained on the ground. When Ronnie had tied his kin on their saddles, Raider moved down with his Peacemaker to fix the cursing Bledman's hands underneath the horse's belly.

"You're gonna pay for this, Pinkerton," Bledman grunted. "Junior'll get you."

Raider leaned over in his face, replying through clenched teeth: "I killed Junior four days ago in Copperhead. Surprise, Ronnie."

"You son of a—"

"Fire in the hole," Doc cried from above.

A red shaft came bouncing down the slope with a short fuse attached to it. The spark burned down into the red before Raider could reach the stick. Raider held his breath, wondering what death was like. Nothing happened. He heard Doc's laughter from above.

"Just a dud," Doc said. "I used the last charge to shake up the rest of Bledman's men."

"I'd like to kill that laughing son of a bitch," Ronnie Bledman hollered.

"Me, too," Raider said, wiping the cold sweat from his face. "Me too."

CHAPTER THREE

Doc and Raider rode down from the northern high country of Montana, following the line of the Rockies toward the rolling hills of the territory's central plain. Behind them they dragged a motley caravan of Bledmans, all tied neatly in their saddles. Raider gave them bread and water once a day, but otherwise they had to remain on horseback. There were just too many of them to allow any freedom of movement.

They had offered Henry a chance to ride along with them, to make the trek to Helena, but he had refused. He had been happy to get back his stock and the money the Bledmans had taken. He didn't see any sense in risking his neck a second time. Raider could see his point.

Ronnie Bledman had screamed at Raider on the first two days of the ride south, but on the third day he had lost his voice and had to be quiet. Raider laughed to himself, keeping his Winchester on his hip. Nobody else gave them any trouble.

A day out of Helena, they picked up a territorial marshal who was glad to see the Bledmans all together. It seemed, the marshal declared, that every one of the Bledmans was wanted for an offense that was punishable by hanging. The marshal asked who would get the reward, and Doc replied that the money should be distributed equally to the families of those murdered by the Bledmans. The marshal said that there wouldn't be much to divvy up, as the Bledmans had ranged far and wide in their killing.

Their caravan attracted a lot of attention as it streamed into Helena. The marshal had to push back the crowd of gawkers so the prisoners could be ushered into the territorial jail. As the Bledmans outnumbered the cells in the jail, the marshal had to incarcerate them three to a room. He said it wouldn't matter, because the Bledmans would be hanged as soon as they constructed a gallows. The hanging tree at the end of town wasn't used anymore. Doc tipped his hat to the marshal and told him that he would receive a synopsis of their report from the home office.

"Look at 'em," Raider said as they left the marshal's office.

The crowd was growing larger.

"Gawkin' like a bunch of Alabama rubberneckers." Raider tipped back his Stetson. "Boy, they really love a hangin'."

Doc straightened his derby. "Don't be so cynical. It's simply the territorial justice system at work."

"Maybe there's a flag around here that we can salute."

"I suggest we try the telegraph office," Doc offered nonchalantly.

Raider stopped dead in the street. Doc turned to look at him. Raider's brow was fretted—a sign that he was angry. He shook his head.

"Now hold on, Doc. We just hit town. Ain't no need to contact the home office right away. I need me a woman and about two days of sleep. And you have to write your reports."

Doc pointed a finger at him. *"Our* reports, Raider."

"I ain't no good at that shit."

Doc threw up his hands. "You really can't be serious about staying in Helena. We've been here before, and there's nothing to the place. Layers of dirt on layers of mud. Not unlike Hell. And if these dilapidated wooden hovels catch fire, the place will be just as hot. Surely you don't want to—"

Raider took off his hat. "Look, Doc, if you don't like Helena, that's your funeral. Besides, don't nobody know we're here yet. There won't be any messages at the telegraph office. Not for us, anyway."

Doc shook his head. "Incorrect. Don't you remember that I told you I wired the home office before we caught up to the Bledmans. I directed them to send any communications to Helena."

"Boy, you sure know how to mess things up." Raider slapped the Stetson on his leg. "You could fuck up a one-horse funeral if you were in the coffin. What you got against me having a good time?"

"It's not your fun that I object to," Doc replied. "It's this dreary mining town. I don't see how this place survived the gold and silver rushes."

Raider put on his hat. "There's a old sayin', Doc: It ain't the house, it's the company you keep. I'll see ya later."

"Where are you going?" Doc called as Raider trekked down the muddy street.

"See you when I've had some shut-eye," Raider called back.

Doc thought about chasing him, but he decided that it wouldn't be worth the effort. Doc wiped his face with his handkerchief. Why was he feeling such a sense of urgency? As much as he loathed Helena, he had never felt so jumpy on his previous visits to the territorial capital. Transporting all these Bledmans had taken a lot out of him. He needed a bath, a good meal, and some sleep.

When Judith was stabled in the livery, Doc strode down the wooden sidewalk toward the Sundowner Hotel. It was a clean establishment run by a chubby widow lady who was always after Doc to make her a wife again. Doc avoided her like the plague, even though he had been tempted more than once by her buxom curves. Raider would have eaten her up with a spoon.

"Perhaps I should visit the Western Union office," Doc said to himself.

As he turned into the telegraph office, Doc felt a hand on his shoulder.

"Sir," said a young man. "I'm Harris, Benjamin Harris of the Helena *Sentinel*. I'm a reporter there."

"Congratulations," Doc said. "I didn't know that Helena

had a paper. I'd appreciate it if you would have a copy delivered to the hotel for me."

"Are you one of those men who brought in the Bledman gang?"

Doc frowned at him. "I am not at liberty to discuss the Bledman case. It's a policy of our agency. Discretion above all."

"But I'd like to know—"

"Good day, sir." Doc pushed past him into the telegraph office.

Harris stayed outside, waiting for Doc to reappear. Doc hoped Harris would find Raider somewhere along the way. He might get a few choice quotes to enliven his readership.

Doc leaned over the counter and regarded the telegraph operator. "Are there any messages for Weatherbee or Raider?"

"Are you really the Pinkerton who brung in the Bledmans?" asked the young man at the telegraph key.

Doc shot him an authoritative glance. "My messages. Immediately."

He didn't like being rude, but he was fatigued and in no mood to deal with the morbid attitudes of the town's citizenry. The telegraph clerk took no offense, but eagerly fetched the telegram that had arrived for Doc. Doc slipped him a nickel for his trouble.

"Thanks," the clerk replied. "Your message just come in this morning."

Doc unfolded the paper. PROCEED AT ONCE TO DENVER. URGENT. AVOID DELAY. FURTHER ORDERS AT WESTERN UNION. ALLAN PINKERTON. Doc's sense of urgency had not been for nothing. AVOID DELAY. And Raider had disappeared, running wild asses all over Helena. Doc would simply have to find him. After a bath and some rest.

The telegraph operator was staring nervously at him. "Are you all right, sir?"

Doc pushed out into the street without a reply. Harris, the reporter, was waiting for him. He was wearing a tasteless checkered suit and a cheap derby. He ran along beside Doc as he strode toward the hotel.

"Aren't you going to tell me anything?" Harris asked.

"Sir," Doc said without breaking stride, "I suggest you try

to find my partner. He's a rather large chap with a scowling face and eyes as black as your derby. He'll tell you everything you want to know."

"Gosh, thanks," Harris said, stopping in the street. "Where is he?"

"I have no idea," Doc replied. "But if you see him, tell him to find me immediately."

Sometimes, Raider thought, Doc was just dead wrong about things. Take Helena, for instance. Doc never dreaded pulling into any place worse than he hated Helena. And Raider had to admit that Helena could be a pretty worm-eaten piece of stew meat. Sometimes it seemed like every scutter-faced saddle tramp north of Colorado ended up in Helena. Of course, that didn't matter if you knew the right place to go—like the little house a mile outside of town. If Doc had known about a place like that, he would have loved to come to Helena, Raider thought.

Raider traded the Appaloosa for a gray gelding and headed out of town. The road was mucky from a heavy spring shower. Bitterroot flowers were popping up along the trail. Raider drank in the air and smiled. If Lolly was available, he might have himself a piss-rippin' afternoon.

"Oh, Miss Lolly," he said out loud. "How I missed you! Whoo-wee!"

He spurred the gray into a gallop, kicking up the mud as he flew down an incline toward the stand of cottonwoods that surrounded Miss Lolly's house. She was round and dark-haired, a bit plump but heavily endowed in the chest and the other areas that Raider liked. He had known her since his young days as a drifter, when they had both been less worn. Raider hadn't seen her in a while, so he wondered if the sparks would fly. But then, they always had flown.

He reined the gelding at the bottom of the hill, slowing into a walk. They always had the same signal. Raider would ride by her house, past the picket fence and the spring garden. She would see him, because a slow rider always attracted attention, even on a busy road. Raider would ride on past the house a ways and then wait for a moment before he turned back to ride by the house again. If she was ready to receive him, there would be a red petticoat in the window.

She had a husband, a rancher who had land below Helena. Raider hoped he might be on spring roundup. If the red petticoat was in the window . . .

"Whoo-wee," Raider said when he saw the crimson undergarment hanging like a curtain behind the smoked panes of glass.

He always rode around to the back entrance, where his mount would not be seen from the road. Lolly didn't have any servants, so there wasn't anyone to spy on them. Raider knew adultery was wrong, but somehow he just couldn't find it in himself to resist Lolly. She had a hell of a lot to offer in the way of knowing how to treat a man.

Her chubby-girl form filled the doorway. "My, my, Raider, you are a scraggly-looking cowboy. You haven't been to see me in ages!"

Raider wondered how many more "visitors" she had besides him. He had asked her once and she had sworn he was her only lover other than her husband. She looked damned good in her white, tight-fitting, high-necked dress, those huge breasts straining at the fabric. Her face was round and pleasant, dark hair piled on top of her head.

Raider toppled out of the saddle. "Lolly, you look like a doggone angel standin' there."

"You're lucky," she replied sweetly. "My hubby left this morning. He'll be driving the herd to market, so he'll be gone for two weeks."

"How'd you like to save a life?"

"Umm, how'd you like to do the same?" She licked her lips.

"Honey," he said. "I need the whole treatment."

"Get over here and kiss me, you saddlebum."

Her lips were thick, brushing his mouth with a wet promise. She smelled of sweet perfume and fancy lip rouge, almost like she had been expecting him. He wrapped her in his arms, pulling her full breasts against his body.

"If I wasn't so grubby I'd have you right here," Raider whispered.

"Now, now," she replied. "You know that when you're under

my roof, you have to do like I say."

He bit her earlobe. "Be good to me, Lolly. I don't have much spunk left in me."

"When have I ever been anything but good to you, Raider?" She slapped his butt. "Now get out of those clothes and get yourself into the bathtub!"

Lolly made him undress right there on the back porch. She was always doing things like that, making Raider do something that sort of embarrassed him. He thought it was funny how sometimes a woman could be meek and submissive, and then at other times she took charge and bossed you around like a kid. When he stepped out of his pants, he saw her brown eyes drop down to his crotch.

Her breast rose and fell. "Lord help me, but I never met a man that was so well blessed. Somebody was thinking of you, Raider, when they made up the word stud."

"Lolly, meanin' no disrespect, but there's a breeze blowin' out here, and I ain't gettin' no warmer." He had goosebumps all over him.

She wrapped her petite hands around his cock.

"I can warm you up," she whispered, rolling his shaft around between her fingers. "Of course, it would be better if you didn't smell like a dead gopher."

"Lolly!" He wanted to take her right there.

She smacked him on the ass with the flat of her palm.

"Get on in there," she said. "I'll get the hot water and the soap."

Raider left his clothes on the porch, entering the house wearing only his Stetson. He slipped his guns into a closet by the kitchen. Lolly wouldn't let him carry them into the bedroom. She was the only woman for whom Raider honored that request.

"You putting your guns in the cupboard, honey?" Lolly called.

He thought she sounded like a dutiful wife. "I sure am, honey."

"These clothes are crusty as a sow. I'll have to boil them over a fire to get them clean. Are you in the tub yet?"

The house was laid out on a simple floor plan—a kitchen, a parlor, a bedroom, and the bathroom. Raider slipped over the wooden floors to the bathroom. He eased himself into the half-filled tub. The water was cool. Raider didn't care. He leaned back and waited for Lolly, who came in shortly carrying a kettle of hot water.

"You must be the luckiest man alive," Lolly said, pouring the water into the tub. "I was going to take a bath myself. I was putting on the kettle when I heard your horse. I'm so glad you remembered our signal."

The warm water eased some of Raider's aches and pains. He was damned tired—until he felt Lolly's soapy hands running along his shoulder. She leaned forward, rubbing his chest and stomach, pressing her breasts into the back of his head.

"Looks like that one-eyed monster's sticking his head out of the water, cowboy. That's some timber."

Raider's erection had broken the surface of the water. Lolly reached down and took it in her hand. She stroked his length with soapy lather. Raider just leaned back and let her play.

"You got a damned big thing, Raider. Biggest one I ever seen. Sometimes when my husband is on top of me I think about you and the way you do me. I get my biscuits just thinking about you."

"Lolly . . ." He needed her next to him.

"I think, can't nobody satisfy me but Raider and his big ax handle." She was breathless. "And then I ask God to forgive me for breaking one of his commandments when you come around. But I guess there's just some things that we ain't meant to resist."

"Why don't you climb in this tub with me, Lolly?"

"Don't go too fast," she replied. "You know I like everything a certain way. Women ain't the same as men."

"I hear you talkin'," Raider replied, leaning back. "You can have it your way, Lolly. I'll just lay back and enjoy it."

"Now that's what I like to hear." She started jerking his prick up and down. "Don't worry, it won't be long."

"Hell, Lolly, it's always long!"

She laughed and poured a bucket of cold water over his head. Raider shivered for a moment, but when he felt her soapy hands on him again, the warmth began to spread through his body. After she had shampooed his coarse head of hair, she dumped a bucket of hot water over him.

"Damn, that feels good," he said.

Lolly grabbed his cock again.

"Time to dry off," she said, trying to pull him up.

"Whoa, woman!" Raider eased himself out of the water.

Lolly went over his broad back with a towel, working her way down to his thighs. When she was on eye-level with his crotch, she toweled his scrotum, carefully inspecting the folds and creases of his masculinity. Raider's legs were growing weaker. He wanted to lie down—with Lolly underneath him.

"Step out of the tub, cowboy. I think you're clean enough."

Raider's feet hit the floor. She dried his calves and his ankles. Then she asked him to sit in a wooden chair in front of the mirror. Lolly trimmed his hair and shaved him. She made him use lilac water and hair tonic. He was as slick as Doc when she got through with him.

"I like my men shining and clean."

Raider grinned. "You like 'em with big pricks, too."

She reached for his genitals, clamping them in her short fingers. "C'mon, honey," she said. "I think it's time for a nap."

As she pulled him toward the bedroom by his cock, Raider wondered why Lolly never said, "Let's go fuck!" It was always "taking a nap" or "Let's lie down for a while." Maybe women just liked everything sugar-coated. Lolly sure was sweet!

"I got a new mattress since you was here last."

Raider flopped down on the clean, starched sheets. He sank into a down mattress. It was about the softest thing he had ever felt. Softer than Lolly's breasts, although not nearly as appealing. She stood in front of him, loosening the buttons of her dress. When the garment fell from her white shoulders, Raider pulled a pillow behind his head and leaned back for the show. For some reason, Lolly always liked to strip in front of him.

"Do you do this for your husband?"

"He doesn't complain," she replied, freeing her breasts from the cumbersome undergarments.

Raider should have felt guilty about topping a married woman, but their infidelity only excited him more. Her clothing hit the floor. She had a little extra baggage on her hips and thighs, but it didn't spoil the picture. She came closer to the bed, her thick lips pursed, her brown nipples erect. Raider couldn't take his eyes off the black wedge between her thighs.

"Move over so I can get in bed," she said softly.

Raider scooted to his left. Lolly slid onto the mattress next to him. Raider started to reach for her.

"No, not yet," she said. "I want to play with you first. I want to torture you until you want me so bad you feel like you're going to die."

Raider could barely catch his breath. "I'm pretty close already."

She just laughed and began to run her hands over his thighs. Her fingers traced a path to his cock. She jerked him with both hands, her lips smiling at the formidable length. Raider cupped her nipples as she worked on his phallus. She put her mouth on him for a second, tasting his flesh, licking his prickhead. But she didn't stay there for long.

"Mind if I put that thing inside me?" she asked.

"I guess you want to get on top."

"I always get my way, Raider. You know that."

She threw a plump leg over him, trapping him on the mattress. Her hips swung over his crotch, and she pressed her bosom into his face. Raider sucked her nipples and tickled her skin with his mustache. Lolly laughed and giggled, keeping her hand on his prick. She worked her hips, guiding the tip of his shaft to the wet entrance of her cunt.

"I want you to fill me up quick," she moaned.

Her hips fell downward. Raider met her motion with an upward thrust. The length of his cock disappeared inside her. She groaned, kissing his mouth, grinding her hips to bring his prick in and out of her. Raider cupped her buttocks, holding on as they shook the featherbed. After a few minutes Lolly stopped moving.

"Slow," she said. "I want to feel it in there. To hold it in there. I want to . . . ahhnn . . ."

He was half in and half out of her. She was gripping the length of his cock with her tight, slippery cunt. Her body trembled, an earthquaking bosom quivering in his face. She gasped for air when Raider pulled her hips downward, impaling her on his shaft.

"I can't stand it!" she whispered hoarsely.

"Let's see if you can stand this."

He rolled her off him, onto her back. Her breasts spilled to both sides of her chest. Raider parted her thighs and positioned himself between them. Lolly grabbed his cockhead and quickly guided it to her wetness. Raider dropped his hips, evoking an unearthly chortle from his plump mistress.

"Damn you, Raider!" she moaned, wrapping her thick legs around his waist. "Hard, cowpoke. Give it to me as hard as you can."

Her face was flushed, her eyes rolled back in her head. Raider rocked in the notch between her legs, driving for his own pleasurable release. Lolly seemed to be enjoying herself as well.

"Give it to me, cowboy. I want to feel it deep."

Raider felt the rising burst. He buried his cock to the hilt, collapsing into Lolly's bosom as he released. An aftershock gripped Lolly's body and she squirmed underneath him. Both of them were covered with perspiration. Lolly laughed at him.

"What's so funny?" he asked.

"I was just thinking that I'm an old sinner."

Raider laughed. "I guess that makes two of us."

He started to roll off her.

"No!" she groaned. "Keep it in there until it gets soft. I want to feel it. It's so damned big."

"Yeah, well, I've learned to live with it," Raider replied. "I wish other women were as like-minded. Some say I hurt them."

"Other women!"

Suddenly he realized he might have said the wrong thing. "Hell, Lolly, I don't—"

"Ooh, you! Get off me."

Raider rolled over to his side of the bed. Lolly slipped under the covers, pulling a comforter over her breasts.

Raider threw up his hands. "Don't tell me you're jealous!"

"Just don't say nothing to me," she replied.

"Oh, then I guess you don't share this bed with your husband," Raider accused. "I guess you don't give him any pussy."

"Hush your foul mouth!"

She rolled over away from him. Raider smiled. He was flattered that Lolly liked to think of him as her personal property. Hell, he thought to himself, if he wasn't in such a dangerous line of work, he might just settle down with someone like her.

"Are there a lot of other women?" Lolly asked softly.

"I don't know, honey. I mean, hell, a man's got to do what it takes to keep himself alive."

"I s'pose I shouldn't be jealous, but I just feel it."

He put his hand on her shoulder. "Now, Lolly, if you don't git over this, I'm not gonna give you that present that I brung you."

She rolled over to face him. "Present?"

"Yeah, right here, sweetheart. Just for you."

He pulled her hand under the covers and guided it to his cock. His rigidity swelled at her touch. Lolly sighed and began to stroke him.

"How's that for a present?"

"Just what I wanted, cowboy. You know how to please me."

Raider settled in between her thighs again. Lolly accepted him, falling back into her orgasmic trance. Raider began to rattle the bedsprings, quickening his motion to bring on his second release. When he had finished, he rolled off her and stretched out with his head on the pillow. Lolly nuzzled his neck, cuddling next to him.

"Tired?"

"Bushed," Raider replied. "I just come off the trail this morning."

"Are you too tired to eat a steak and some of my scalloped potatoes?"

Raider licked his lips. "How about some homemade bread and butter."

"I just churned up a dish this morning."

"Yeah, I guess there ain't no milk shortage around here." He was looking at her breasts.

"Oh, Raider. How you do go on! Now, you just take a little nap and I'll whip up some supper."

She jiggled out of bed and into a soft robe. Raider pulled the covers over his body and settled his head into the feather pillow. He could still feel her wetness on him. As he started to drift off, the smell of frying onions reached his nose. He hoped she would let him sleep before she started her games again.

• • •

Doc sat at the breakfast table reading a copy of the Helena *Sentinel*. Benjamin Harris, the young scrivener, had used a great deal of artistic license in portraying their capture of the Bledman gang. He described a vague but punchy gunfight that had Doc and Raider gunning down Lyle Bledman as he sprayed the air with his final burst of lead. According to Harris, the other Bledmans had given up, as they were grief-stricken over Lyle's untimely death.

Doc could only laugh at the misrepresentation of the facts. He had considered filing a complaint with the home office when he mailed in his finished reports. He finally decided against it. He couldn't be concerned about the Bledman case with the message from the home office hanging over his head. Where the hell was Raider?

"More coffee, Mr. Weatherbee?" asked Mrs. Hopkins, the hotel's proprietor.

Doc nodded at her, careful not to smile too warmly.

Mrs. Hopkins was still a handsome woman, but Doc didn't want to encourage her. Not that she wouldn't have been a fine catch, especially after her husband had been kind enough to leave her the hotel in his will. But Doc knew that a proper woman like Mrs. Hopkins would want one thing from a man— a wedding ring.

Mrs. Hopkins hovered at his side. "Are the eggs satisfactory, Mr. Weatherbee?"

Her eyes were a glorious shade of green. Doc looked into his steaming coffee cup. He had to fight the smell of her cologne.

"The eggs were fine," Doc replied. "I'm a bit preoccupied today."

He thought about the telegram in his coat pocket.

"Perhaps you should attend prayer meeting with me tonight," she offered. "A session with the good book can lessen your burden."

Doc shifted nervously in his chair. "Well, if I'm free, perhaps I can."

"Then I can count on you attending?" Her green eyes indicted him.

"If all goes well," he replied. "My partner may arrive, but

if I am free, then I certainly will be glad to escort you to prayer meeting."

She beamed with a smiling face and bright eyes. Doc sipped his coffee, which was quite good by any standards. As she walked away from him, Doc glanced out the window, watching for Raider. If he didn't arrive in time, Doc would have to make up another excuse to get out of the prayer meeting.

Raider felt Lolly next to him before he opened his eyes. Her skin was warm and slightly moist. His cock was hard with a morning erection. He was still half asleep as he impaled her. She woke up to her pleasure, moaning as the sun filled the room. When they were finished, Lolly got up and drew back the curtains. Her face shone in the morning light.

"Looks like we didn't hear the rooster, cowboy."

Raider turned lazily under the warm comforter. "The rooster don't give a damn, Lolly."

"Breakfast, dear?" She loved to feed her men.

"How about five eggs with ham, some biscuits, and a quart of milk?"

"Are you forgetting my red-eye gravy?"

Raider threw back the covers. "Hell, girl, dish it up. I'm starvin'."

She shook her finger at him. "You can't eat buck naked. Your clothes are on the back porch. I washed them last night, after you started snoring. They should be dry by now."

Raider followed her into the kitchen. He found his clean clothes and slipped into them. Lolly sure as hell knew how to spoil a man. Her husband was a lucky boy, Raider thought. Even if she couldn't be trusted while he was away. By the time he put his boots on, Lolly had breakfast on the table.

"Shore is good," Raider said, sopping up the ham gravy with a biscuit. "Maybe we should—"

"Shh." She seemed suddenly frightened.

"Lolly, what the hell is it?" He didn't like the look in her eyes.

She left the room for a minute. Raider peered down the hall to see her looking out the front window. Then he heard jangling harnesses. Lolly came flying back into the kitchen, her eyes filled with terror.

"My husband's come back!" she cried, urging him up from the table.

Raider almost gagged on a piece of ham. He knocked over his chair as he rose from the table. Lolly told him to get his guns out of the closet where he had placed them the day before. As Raider secured his arms, he realized that he sure as hell didn't feel like shooting it out with a jealous husband. Lolly pushed his Stetson down on his head.

"Ride out the back way," she said. "You can head south until you hit a stream. Follow it back into Helena."

She kissed him one last time.

"Sorry, cowboy. Maybe we'll have better luck next time. You better hurry."

The rattling harnesses stopped. Raider bolted out the back door, jumping into the saddle of the gray. He spurred the animal and pounded away from the house. When he reached the small stream, he turned back to make sure no one was following him. He thought he saw dust on the crest of the hill above him. Was it from his own horse? He slipped his rifle into the scabbard on the saddle and then buckled his holster around him. As he rode hard for town, he wondered if he would have to use his Colt. It would be a long time before he visited Lolly again.

Doc stood up from the table when he saw his partner barreling down the street on the gray. Raider tied off the reins and then stomped into the Sundowner. The widow Hopkins cast a wary eye toward the big man from Arkansas. Doc managed to intercede before Raider tangled with her.

"Pay no attention to him, Mrs. Hopkins," Doc said. Then to Raider: "Where the devil have you been?"

Raider pulled him aside. "Doc, I think we better get the hell out of Helena before trouble starts."

"It just so happens that we've received a telegram directing us to Denver on urgent business."

"Hell, Doc, I'm ready. Where's your damned mule?"

"At the livery."

"I'll go get her, then," Raider said, starting for the door.

"Raider, why are you suddenly in such a hurry?"

"No reason," Raider replied. "I'll be back here in a half hour."

Doc stopped him. "Woman trouble?"

Raider pointed a finger at him. "You just be ready to ride when I get back."

Doc laughed. Raider had to be in dire straights to actually *volunteer* to put Judith in harness. Ordinarily, he hated Doc's mule. As Doc turned back toward the stairs, he caught the widow glaring at him.

The widow's hands were on her hips. "Honestly, some of the company you keep!"

Spoken like a true wife, Doc thought.

"I'm afraid that I have no choice, Mrs. Hopkins. He was assigned to work with me by the home office."

The disappointment was evident in the widow's lovely face. "When will you be leaving?"

"I have to check out this morning," He tried to sound let down.

"I don't suppose you'll be attending prayer meeting with me," she said with an eyebrow raised.

"Forgive me, dear friend. But I have most urgent business."

"We're going to pray for the souls of those poor men you brought to justice," said Mrs. Hopkins. "They are going to be hanged after all."

Doc just bowed and swept up the stairs without answering her. He didn't think it prudent that he pray for the souls of the Bledmans. After all, he was directly responsible for sending them to the gallows.

CHAPTER FOUR

They headed southeast, away from Helena and the Rockies, toward the low-lying central plains of Wyoming and Colorado. Doc noticed that Raider kept looking over his shoulder, casting wary glances behind them. It didn't take much thinking for Doc to figure out that Raider was watching for a jealous husband. But he didn't say anything to the big man from Arkansas. They traveled in silence, trying to make good time in light of Allan Pinkerton's urgent message. On the fourth day out of Helena they crossed the Colorado border, near the woodlands of Medicine Bow.

"We should be in Denver by tomorrow night," Doc said.

"You want to ride on through or make camp?" Raider cast a wary glance toward the forest.

Doc drank in the fresh air. "I'd prefer to camp."

"Why?" Raider still stared at the forest.

"Well, it would be better to arrive in Denver fit and fresh," Doc offered. "And this may be the last chance to rest before we're back on a case."

Raider grumbled and looked away from his partner.

"What's the matter?"

"I ain't in love with that forest yonder," Raider replied.

Doc shook his head. "Still spooked. I swear, your superstitions can be very annoying, Raider."

"Yeah, well, I don't want some sidewinder sneakin' up on me and cold-cockin' me when I ain't lookin'."

"A jealous husband sidewinder?"

Raider scowled at his partner. "You're too smart sometimes, Doc."

They rode along in silence, like two people who know practically everything about each other but are unable to communicate. Doc could not suppress his devilish smirk. He enjoyed needling Raider.

"Don't let your guilt get the best of you, Raider."

"Aw hell," Raider muttered. "Why you so dead set on campin' anyway?"

"Up ahead, about five miles, there's a small creek that runs along the edge of the forest. In the middle of that creek there's a trout pool of rainbows and cutthroats that poses the ultimate challenge for an angler of—"

"You mean all this commotion is just because you want to do some fishin'?"

"Precisely," Doc replied. "I enjoy angling immensely."

"Well, if Pinkerton chews out our asses because we're late, then don't blame me."

Raider spurred the gray and rode ahead of the wagon. Doc reached into his pocket and pulled out a cheroot. He torched the end of the stogie and blew out a puff of smoke. Stopping to camp for one night was not out of line at all, he thought. They had ridden through the darkness for three evenings without a break. Even Allan Pinkerton could not expect them to sustain their superhuman efforts.

Doc took in a breath of fresh air. Spring had arrived on the plain, prompting the emergence of multicolored blossoms. It felt good to be alive on such a day. And the world would not end if they arrived in Denver a few hours late.

Raider thought it uncharacteristic of Doc to sacrifice precious time for his own pleasure. Not that he was complaining. The crystal clear stream was shaded by the pines and junipers overhead. A pebble-paved bank was the perfect resting spot for someone who had been in the saddle for half a week. The damned spring air was getting to them, Raider thought, making both of them lazy. Maybe Doc had been right about camping for an afternoon and a night. A good rest would prepare them for what lay ahead.

"Anything bitin'?" Raider called to Doc, who stood in mid-stream with his trousers rolled up to his knees.

"Quiet, Raider, you'll scare the fish."

Raider liked to wet a line as good as anybody, but it seemed like an awful lot of work the way Doc did it. Doc had spent the better part of an hour searching for a stick and then stripping it down to accommodate his cotton fishing line. He also had a weird-looking contraption that he used to retrieve the line, and instead of a worm on the end of a hook, he preferred to tempt the trout with something that he called "flies." Doc had a city-boy way of complicating things that sometimes irritated Raider. This time, however, Raider enjoyed gloating as Doc's hook came back empty.

"I didn't know trout ate a bunch of red feathers with a piece of wire inside," Raider called. "Maybe I ought to dig you some wigglers or some night crawlers."

"Raider," Doc said, casting his line. "If you'd please be—"

The clear water erupted where Doc had dropped the fly. He pulled back on his fishing pole, hooking the huge rainbow that rolled in the brook. Raider could not believe his eyes. He sat up in the shade and watched as Doc played the trout. Suddenly Raider was ready for a supper of fresh fish.

"Get him, Doc!" He jumped up to watch. "Whoo-wee, that's a big 'un."

Doc took his time, letting the trout tire against the leverage of the rod. It would probably weigh out at eight pounds, Doc thought. He had caught bigger, but never one that had fought more. As he was reaching down to lift the trout, the fish made another run away from him.

"Don't lose him, Doc," Raider called. "If he's—"

The water frothed again. Doc's line went slack. A shotgun had gone off. Someone had blasted the trout off his hook. Raider reached for his Colt.

A loathsome voice cut through the afternoon air. It came

from the trees, where the smoke from the shotgun was settling. "Don't try it, big man. Dandy, get out of the water and walk toward your partner."

Raider's hand hesitated over his holster.

"Go on," said the voice. "We got five guns on you, Pinkerton. You move a' inch and you'll die sooner than you think."

Raider gritted his teeth. "Damn it, I knew it was a mistake to stop here."

"Steady," Doc said as he waded out of the stream. "We aren't dead yet. Let's see what they want first."

The man in the trees barked his orders. "Drop that hog leg, boy. Use your left hand and don't make no quick moves."

"Dad-burn it, Doc, you and me is slippin'. We let 'em get the drop on us like a couple of greenhorn kids."

His holster hit the bank of the stream. Doc stood next to him with his feet still bare. Five men moved down out the trees, holding rifles and shotguns. They looked like hard trail-riders in their felt hats and slickers. Raider wondered if they were just thieves or if they had a personal grudge.

A chunky man with a shotgun seemed to be the leader. "Well, well. Looks like I done snuck up on Doc Weatherbee and his big ape Raider."

"Please identify yourself, sir," Doc said.

"Eye-dent-ti-fie!" The man howled with laughter. "Hear that, boys? He wants to 'eye-dent-ti-fie' us."

The four other men laughed too. Raider considered diving for his Colt, going out with a blaze of glory, taking as many of them as he could before the shotgun sent him to his reward. He decided to wait for the right moment.

"You meanin' that you don't know who I am?" asked the man with the shotgun. "Look close, Doc. See any family resemblance?"

Doc's eyes bulged with recognition. "Bledman!"

"Bubba Bledman," cried the man with the shotgun. "You done killed all my clan. Sent 'em to hang. Now I'm gonna pay you back."

"You the last of the Bledmans?" Raider asked.

"What's it to you, big man?"

"Let's hang him, Bubba," said one of Bledman's henchmen. "Let's string him up the way they did Ronnie and Lyle."

Raider bristled. "Lyle wasn't hanged."

Bledman got up in his face. "You mean one of my brothers escaped?"

Raider smirked. "No, I done killed him. And I shot Junior, too. And I'm glad I done it. Now what do you think about that?"

Doc could not believe that Raider was provoking them. He stood there wide-eyed, thinking that he was going to die without his shoes on. Bledman's men closed in tighter.

"We gonna string 'em up, Bubba?"

"No," Bledman replied. "I'm gonna shoot 'em both right now. We don't want to give 'em a chance to try no tricks. I'm gonna let 'em have it right between the eyes."

He broke the shotgun in half and slipped in two brass shells.

"Been nice knowin' you, Doc."

"Raider, if you could reach your pistol . . ."

Bledman raised the shotgun. "Ain't nobody reachin' nothin'. I'm sendin' you on to be with my kin that you killed."

He thumbed back the twin hammers on the scattergun. Raider was tensing to dive for his Colt when Bledman's body buckled and fell forward. The shotgun exploded harmlessly into the ground. Bledman's men looked around, toward the trees. As they aimed their rifles into the forest, Raider heard whooshing sounds in the air. Bledman's four men fell to the ground, as dead as their leader. Indian arrows were lodged in their bodies.

"Son of a bitch," Raider stared at the shaft in Bubba's back.

Doc started for the Colt on the ground. Raider grabbed his arm to stop him. "Be still, Doc."

"But—"

"Don't move."

"Do you want to die?" Doc cried.

"We'd be dead right now if somebody in them trees wanted us to be." Raider peered into the shadows of the forest. "All right, come on down, partner. We want to thank you for savin' our lives."

A breeze seemed to move through the trees. A man's body flew out of the forest, into the stream. Two more men followed him. They were wearing tanned skins for trousers. All three of them were bare-chested.

"Arapaho," Raider said softly to Doc.

"Do you think they're hostile?"

Two of the Arapaho braves were carrying bows. The big one, obviously the leader, was wearing an old Navy Colt in a holster. He also sported a stovepipe hat with an eagle feather in the band. Doc and Raider watched as the warrior reached into the stream and plucked out the shattered carcass of the trout that Bubba Bledman had blasted. He cried out and slung the waste back into the trees.

"Apparently he doesn't approve of Bledman's method of angling," Doc said.

"After what the white man has done to his tribe, he probably don't approve of a goddamn thing we do." Raider studied the pistol. "I bet he took that Colt off a dead soldier."

The Arapaho braves started toward Doc and Raider.

"Shouldn't you try your pistol?" Doc asked.

Raider shook his head. "Let him come on. Let's see what he wants."

"But I wholeheartedly think that——"

"Like I said, if he wanted us dead, we'd be layin' there next to Bubba Bledman." Raider was trying hard to keep his hands from shaking.

When the Indians stood toe to toe with them, Raider saw that they were definitely not a war party. They weren't wearing paint, and three Arapaho would never go out looking for trouble by themselves. Maybe they were renegades who wanted to be left alone, living back in the hills and forests with their squaws. Moving on every time they caught the smell of white men on the wind. Raider peered into eyes that were as black as his own.

"How do," Raider said, smiling.

The brave smiled and looked up at Raider's Stetson.

"I do believe he's admiring your hat," Doc said. "Why don't you offer it to him?"

"Hell, Doc, I just——"

"Do it, man!"

Raider took off his hat and offered it to the brave. He took it and placed it on his head. In turn, he offered the stovepipe hat to Raider.

"Take it and put it on your head," Doc urged.

"Hell, Doc, sometimes these Injuns got head lice."

"Just do it."

Raider put the stovepipe hat on his head. The Indian leader laughed and stepped over next to Doc. Doc immediately took off his derby and offered it to him. He refused.

Raider chuckled. "Hell, Doc, he hates your hat. That Injun has style."

"He's admiring my fishing gear."

Doc was still holding the makeshift pole. He smiled and offered the rig to the Arapaho leader. "You can have it, sir. In exchange for our lives."

The Indian howled with delight, showing the pole to his men. Doc and Raider looked at each other. Raider shrugged his shoulders.

"I guess that's why he didn't kill *us*. He must've admired the way you fished."

The brave turned back toward Doc. He drew his Navy Colt. Doc's face turned two shades of white. The brave offered Doc the Colt's handle.

Doc shook his head. "No thank you, sir. I don't want your pistol."

The Indian looked puzzled for a moment. Then he ripped a pendant from around his neck. He held it out to Doc. It was a bear claw that had been strung on a leather thong. The tip of the claw had been dipped in red paint.

Raider leaned over. "Take it, Doc. You don't want to piss off this ole boy."

"Well, I suppose not, but I . . ."

Raider frowned. "This is Red Clay, Doc, and that's his most prized possession in his hand. He took that claw off a bear he killed himself. Probably with a bow and arrow."

Doc accepted the pendant from Red Claw, who howled again and took one last look at Doc and Raider. Then he motioned to his men and they were moving into the woods again, sliding between tree trunks like three phantom deer. Raider heaved a sigh of relief and took off the stovepipe.

"We was pretty lucky there."

Doc's hands were wet. "Yes, I suppose we were fortunate."

"Red Claw was a great chief in his day. Rumor had it that he was dead, but he must be holin' up hereabouts."

"For a dead man, he drives a hard bargain." Doc examined the Indian trinket in his hands.

Raider stared at the trees. "Let's vamoose now, Doc. It's gettin' dark, and this place done spooked me out. I'll shoot somethin' for dinner. Let's just git rollin'."

"Raider?" Doc was not looking at him.

"Yeah, Doc."

Doc's head was hanging. "It was a mistake to stop here. I apologize for the lapse. I'll never subject you again to..."

Raider shrugged it off. "Put a cork in it, Doc. I ain't one to rub salt in a wound. Grab your shoes and let's head for Denver. We ain't got time for no widow-lady confessions."

Doc looked at the dead men. "What about them? I mean, we have to bury them and write a report."

Raider snorted like a bull. "Hell, Doc, we didn't kill 'em." He hopped into the saddle of the gray. "Come on, Doc, before we—"

"Raider, I refuse to leave with these dead men lying here."

"Aw, hell," Raider grunted, climbing down again. "Git your damn shovel. We ain't got time to argue."

As Raider dug in the soft sand along the streambed, he kept a watchful eye on the woods. The way he figured it, they still owed Red Claw their lives. But as far as Raider was concerned, he didn't care if he ever saw Red Claw again. He wasn't the kind of man you wanted to be indebted to.

Again they were silent as they rode by starlight through the night. Daybreak seemed to stir a warm wind on the plain, a soft palm of air that made Raider languid. Doc was brooding about the incident with the final Bledman brother. Doc wasn't used to making mistakes.

"I been thinkin', Doc," Raider said. "Bubba probably picked up our trail right outside Helena. He got word about what we done, so he laid for us."

"Raider..."

"Hell, shut up a minute, Doc. You ain't the only one in this world who knows everything about everything. If you didn't have your head in the sand, you'd see that Bubba would've hit us anyway. Only he might not of done it while Red Claw was sittin' over us like a guardian angel. You actually saved us by stoppin' there. I mean, we were none too smart, but you followed your instincts and it turned out right."

Doc sat up. "Yes," he said slowly. "I suppose I did."

"So we don't need to run this thing into the ground. See what I mean? We just buried five bad boys who was killed by a renegade Indian."

"Raider, you have a remarkable ability to put things in perspective." Doc was starting to perk up.

"Take the roll of the dice and live with it, partner."

Doc laughed and shook his head.

"No report either, Doc." Raider cast a sideways glance at his partner.

After a moment of thought, Doc replied, "All right. No report."

Raider almost fell out of his saddle. Doc usually wrote a report on everything. Like he enjoyed it!

"This Bledman thing is officially closed, then," Raider said.

"Fine by me."

"You want me to shoot somethin' for breakfast?"

"We should arrive in Denver in time for lunch," Doc replied. "Can you wait?"

"I can if you can."

Doc shook the reins. "We wait."

Raider was glad that Doc's spirit had returned. It was always better to be in a good mood when you were starting a new case. A sullen man spent too much time thinking about his troubles. He might not be able to cover you the next time you met a shotgun in the woods.

Doc and Raider both liked Denver. The mile-high town was situated perfectly in the crux of the Rocky Mountain region. As the state capital, Denver supported a thriving legal community and regional politics. Cattle and lumber moved down from the northern ranges and forests, on their way south and east. Of course, the real contributors to Denver's development were gold and silver, the two elements that accounted for a great deal of western migration. It was all sort of exciting for two men who had been traipsing through the wilds of the north country.

"I wonder if Little Bright Wing is still in town?" Raider said as they rolled down Denver's main thoroughfare.

Little Bright Wing was an Indian prostitute who had crossed their paths—and Raider's bedroll. Doc could see that Raider's thoughts were already turning to women. Next he would be wanting some whiskey and a poker game. Doc knew how he felt. There was someone special for Doc in Denver—if she was still in town, that is. He hadn't seen her in quite some time.

"I reckon I could take a look around that house where she used to work." Raider was peering toward the edge of town. "You want to come along?"

"We're going directly to the Western Union office," Doc insisted. "I want to follow procedure from here on out."

Raider remembered the incident at the stream. "I hear you, Doc."

The telegram was waiting for them under Doc's name. They were directed to see a Mr. Hobert Bixley of the Medicine Bow Silver Company, 12 Silver Street. They were to report as soon as possible. Doc quickly penned a message for the home office to report that they were in motion on the case. Raider could see that his partner was ready to tackle a problem, something that needed solving. It was best that they got right to it.

Raider slapped his thigh. "I reckon Little Bright Wing will have to wait."

"For now," Doc replied.

When Judith and the gray were stabled in the livery, they pounded the wooden sidewalk to Silver Street. The offices of the Medicine Bow Silver Company comprised half the block. Doc and Raider pushed through the heavy oak door into an ornate parlor. The decorations suggested a woman's touch, Doc thought. Raider thought it looked like a cathouse parlor. A stiff, formal young man stood up behind his desk and greeted them.

"May I help you, sirs?"

"We've been summoned by Hobert Bixley," Doc replied.

"We are representatives of the Pinkerton National Detective Agency."

"Yes, certainly," the man replied, his formality vanishing instantly. "I'll tell him you are here."

He left and returned before Doc and Raider could exchange their opinions of the Medicine Bow offices. They were ushered down a long hall, into a room that appeared to be a library. Books covered the walls, and a redwood desk dominated half the room. They were left alone to sit in two plush chairs in front of the desk.

Raider was impressed by the interior. "This Bixley must have a few pesos."

"Business certainly appears to be good," Doc rejoined.

"You wouldn't say that if you had spoken to me," said a voice from behind them.

Doc rose and turned toward the voice. A small, wrinkled gentleman stood in the threshold of the library door. Wire-rimmed spectacles teetered on the end of his nose. He hobbled when he walked, slowly coming around to take his place by the desk. His face had been ravaged by time, but his voice carried a certain benevolent quality, Doc thought. He wore a dark suit that made him look like a hideous schoolboy to Raider.

"Gentlemen," he said. "I am Hobert Bixley, owner and president of this mining company."

Doc shook his hand. "I am Doc Weatherbee. And this is my partner, Raider. I'm sorry that we took so long getting here, but we were delayed with some ghastly business north of here."

"I didn't mind the wait, Weatherbee. I told Allan Pinkerton I wanted his two best men to deal with this case."

Raider's face showed a half grin. "That's us."

"Pay no attention to my partner's lack of modesty," Doc said. "How may we be of assistance, Mr. Bixley?"

Bixley leaned back and folded his hands.

"Gentlemen, I have two mining operations right now. One in Wyoming and one here in Colorado. I am not concerned with the Wyoming operation. Things are running smoothly there. We aren't bringing in much in the way of silver, but we discovered a thick vein of lead that's producing a great deal of income."

He coughed and cleared his throat. He seemed to be having

trouble breathing. After a moment he composed himself and went on. "It's the Colorado mine that's giving me fits."

Raider wanted to spur him on. "What seems to be the trouble?"

Bixley sighed. "It's the miners. They won't work the mines. My operation has been closed down completely."

"I'm afraid we've come for nothing," Doc replied. "Our agency will not engage in disputes between employers and employees. Problems of labor are not in our..."

Bixley's eyes were pleading. "Sir, allow me to finish. I don't want you to get the miners to go back to work. They aren't refusing to work because they're angry with the company. They aren't working because they are frightened right out of their skins."

"Frightened?" Doc studied the fretful gentleman's face.

Bixley ran a rough hand over his thin hair. "I don't know how to tell you this without sounding like a fool," he said. "The men won't go into the mine because they say it's haunted."

Raider's smile had vanished. "Haunted?"

Doc glared at him. "Raider, your manner does not have to be—"

"No, don't chastise him, Mr. Weatherbee," Bixley said. "I had the same reaction when the news was brought to me."

Doc's interest was growing. He leaned forward. "Do you have reason to believe that the mine *is* haunted?"

"Again I will sound the fool," Bixley replied. "There have been reports of supernatural occurrences. Ghosts, devils, demons from Hell."

"And your boys have seen this stuff?" Raider asked.

"I swear to you, I have a foreman, a man who has been with me for ten years. He claims to have seen fire belching from the mountain. He claims that Satan himself appeared in the mine shaft." It tired him to talk about it.

Doc leaned in a little. "What is this foreman's name?"

"Lutrell."

Raider's black eyes were skeptical. "Does this Lutrell drink?"

"As much as any, I suppose," Bixley replied. "But I would vouch for his character and his reliablilty. I would trust him with my own life."

Doc's face was serious. "I think the only thing for us to do is to take a look at the haunted mine."

"Doc," Raider whispered. "Don't joke around about nothin' like this. I think we ought to wire the home office before we take off huntin' spooks."

"Does Allan Pinkerton know why you've asked for us?" Doc asked Bixley.

"Yes," Bixley replied. "I told him about the reports from the mine. He said that you two were the right men to be assigned to the case."

"We get all the shit work," Raider muttered.

"Raider, Mr. Bixley doesn't want to—"

"No matter," Bixley said with an ironic laugh. "I would feel the same way in Raider's place. This whole thing has made me a bit loco. I am anxious to have it resolved."

"Are there any other circumstances pertinent to the case?" Doc asked.

"Such as?"

"Has anyone been injured?"

Bixley shook his head. "But . . . you are both going to think me as senile as I look when I tell you the rest."

"Try us," Raider said.

"My foreman reports that silver is disappearing from the veins, even though the men are not working the mines. He has inspected the mine during the daylight hours. Someone has been taking out the silver without anyone seeing them. My foreman believes that close to fifteen thousand dollars worth of silver has disappeared in the last month."

Raider met Doc's gaze. "I ain't never heard of no spook needin' silver."

"I daresay a ghost would not be able to carry out fifteen thousand dollars worth of precious ore." Doc said. "Mr. Bixley, you look dubious."

"I suppose I should tell you quickly." He braced himself. "It happened a long time ago, when I was still a prospector. My former partner and I were scouting the site where we're now working. We established this company together. Both of us were along in years, and we had both left our families to join in the silver rush. You can imagine how we felt when we finally struck it rich." His exhausted voice trailed off.

"You said 'former' partner." Doc was trying to lead him along.

"Lymon Partridge. He died accidentally. About a year ago. I knew him all my life. Part of a mine shaft collapsed on top of him. He left me everything in his will, as his wife was dead and his only brother had gone on to parts unknown. He had a son for whom I searched in vain."

Raider's eyes had narrowed. "You mean he left you the whole kit and caboodle?"

"Everything." Bixley looked at both of them. His face sagged.

"So you benefited from his death." Doc's tone was not accusing.

"That raised quite a few eyebrows in the territory," Bixley said. "Some say that I was responsible for his death. You see, I was supposed to be with him when he inspected the shaft, but I had been detained in Cheyenne."

Raider leaned back in his chair. "You got to admit that it don't look too good for you."

"I swear before God that I did not have anything to do with Lymon's death," Bixley replied. "He was a good man. I was saddened when he died."

"So you think your old partner has come back to haunt the mine?" Raider wore a dubious smirk.

"I don't know what to think," Bixley replied. "I simply entreat you gentlemen to look into the case and let me know about your findings."

"We certainly have our work cut out for us," Doc said.

"Then you'll accept the case?" Bixley was hopeful for the first time.

Doc nodded. "Of course. But I will need a certain amount of cooperation from you, Mr. Bixley."

"What can I do for you, sir?" The old man was suddenly eager to help.

"First, I will need maps of your mining operations showing all of the tunnels and the layout of the landscape. Also, it would be helpful if you would provide us with a list of your employees—past and present—for the last five years. And I would like a map showing us the route to your Colorado operation."

"Done," Bixley said. "I will have everything for you tomorrow morning."

"Make sure you include the reports that deal with the occurrences at the mine in question." Doc was already making notes on a piece of paper.

"Don't you mean 'supernatural occurrences'?"

"No," Doc replied. "I do not believe in ghosts, sir. I believe that these things can be explained and linked to the disappearance of the silver."

"I admire your confidence and enthusiasm."

Raider wasn't so sure he admired his partner. "Doc, don't you think we ought to check with the home office on this? Meanin' no disrespect to Mr. Bixley here, but this sounds kinda crazy to me. Maybe the state marshal oughta take a look first."

"The state marshal laughed my foreman out of his office," Bixley rejoined.

"Pay no attention to my partner," Doc said. "We're going to pursue this investigation, Mr. Bixley. However, I must reiterate the fact that we cannot take part in any dispute between you and your employees. Is that understood?"

Bixley nodded. "I understand, sir. Now, if you need accommodations while you are in Denver, I have plenty of room over the offices."

"That won't be necessary," Doc replied. "But you might suggest a hotel where we can stay."

"The Missoula. It's clean and comfortable. When you sign in, have everything billed to me. I insist on picking up the expense."

Doc rose from his chair. "As you wish, Mr. Bixley."

"Gentlemen," Bixley said, rising behind his desk, "I wish you good luck in your investigation. If you are successful, you may very well lift the dark cloud that hangs over my family."

"I assure you, Mr. Bixley," replied Doc, "that we will do our best."

When they were on the sidewalk again, Raider shook his head. "Doc, this sounds like a bunch of bullshit to me."

"Could it be that you don't like the idea of chasing after ghosts?" Doc chuckled. "You are superstitious after all."

"Let's just say that I've seen some things in my life that nobody could explain."

"Raider, man's ignorance can only be dispelled when he seeks the truth."

"Yeah, well, I don't know about none of that stuff, but old Bixley there seems to be a little nervous about somethin'." Raider scowled. "I think maybe he's got somethin' to hide."

"A clever observation—although he was perfectly honest with us about his partner's death."

"He mighta told us so he wouldn't look bad when we found out on our own," Raider offered.

Doc rasied his hand. "Forget Bixley, Raider. Aren't you curious about the reports of devils and demons?"

"Curious? Hell, you think I like that spirit stuff? That's for Injuns and Gypsy fortune-tellers. Give me a good gunfight any day. At least you know what you're up against then."

"Would you like me to wire the home office and find another partner?"

"You mean you'd do that?"

"Well, if you're afraid of a few ghost stories . . ."

Raider bristled. "Whoa! I ain't afraid o' nothin'."

"Then I suggest you get a good night's sleep, and we can start fresh tomorrow," Doc said bluntly.

They were standing in front of the hotel.

Raider took off his hat and hit it. "How come we never get a case that's normal?"

"We'd be bored with anything else."

Raider twirled his hat. "Have you still got that bear claw that our Injun buddy gave us?"

"Yes, it's in my coat pocket," Doc replied. "Why?"

"It's big medicine," Raider said. "Give it to me, so I can keep it."

"Why do you want it?"

Raider held out his hand. "Just give it to me."

"Not until you tell me why you want it."

"Hell, Doc, I know you don't believe in all of this mumbo-jumbo, and I hate to see that Injun charm goin' to waste."

"Heap big magic." Doc tossed the pendant to Raider.

Raider dropped the bear claw into his boot and started down the sidewalk away from Doc.

"Where are you going?" Doc called.

"To see if I can find Little Bright Wing."

"You're not going to stay at the hotel?"

"Not if the cathouse is open."

"Be at Bixley's first thing in the morning," Doc shouted. "No later than eight o'clock."

Raider waved back to him. Doc looked across the street at the hotel. He didn't feel like staying there either. He had a woman on his mind. He would prefer staying with her, if she was still in Denver.

CHAPTER FIVE

Doc waited for her under a cottonwood tree at the end of the street. He watched the one-room schoolhouse, sitting under the rustling leaves, admiring the spring day. He realized he had dozed off when the school bell rang and the joyous children ran from the bright red building, their cries resounding through the crisp air. Doc felt as if he had awakened in a dream. Kathryn appeared at the window for an instant, wearing a high-necked beige dress that made her look like an angel. Thick spectacles covered her soft face, and her brownish-blond tresses were rolled into a bun on the back of her aristocratic head. Doc knew from experience that she was not the old-maid schoolteacher known by the community of Denver.

She didn't see Doc, but turned back into the schoolhouse. Doc couldn't believe the way his heart was pounding. He felt like a young schoolboy about to take an apple to the school-marm, his object of infatuation. With his derby in hand, he walked slowly through the gate in the white picket fence, along the path that led up to the school steps. Doc stood in the threshold with his face obscured by the afternoon shadows.

How would she react when she knew it was he? Their last parting had not been a pleasant one.

"I'm looking for the schoolmarm," Doc said. "I believe my son is having trouble with mathematics."

Kathryn stood up behind the desk. She adjusted her spectacles on her nose. The poor lady was blind without them. Her blue eyes were magnified by the lenses.

"I don't know you, sir."

"My son Johnny is in your class."

"Johnny McKinney? But he isn't having trouble with his arithmetic. Why, he's one of my . . . Wait, you aren't Johnny's father. Johnny's father was killed last year. Who . . . ? Your voice. Doc, is it really you?"

"I knew I couldn't fool you for long."

Kathryn rushed toward Doc and wrapped him in her slender arms. She was crying. Doc directed her back to her desk, where he eased her into a wooden chair. He went down on one knee and kissed the back of her hand. She removed her glasses and looked down at him with tearful eyes.

"I was hoping God would send me something."

"My entrance is far from providential," Doc replied softly. "Whatever is bothering you, my dear girl?"

"Oh, Doc, I don't want to say. Lately I've been fretting so I can hardly stand to get out of bed in the morning."

"Is the Citizens' Committee still harassing you about moving out on your own?"

The town dignitaries had frowned when Kathryn had left her aunt's house to live alone. It was scandalous for a young lady, a schoolteacher at that, to live by herself. They had threatened her job, but Kathryn had endured.

"Yes, they're coming at me again," Kathryn replied. "And they're using the state to do it."

Doc stood up and leaned against the desk. "Elaborate for me," he said. "Perhaps I can assist you."

"Oh, damn this statehood. Everything was fine when we were a territory. But now the legislature has created an education commission to regulate all the schools in the state. They're going to license teachers. Can you believe it? And because I haven't attended college, I may lose my job."

"Then I can assume all teachers need some college training to receive this license."

"Yes," she replied. "The Citizens' Committee offered to pay for my college back east and to vouch for me with the education commission. Only I have to move back in with my aunt first."

"Damned if you do, damned if you don't. Kathryn, I have a little money, about two hundred dollars, in a bank in San Francisco. I'd love to give you more, but I send most of my pay back home, to our family trust in Boston, otherwise I'd—"

"Shush, you, Weatherbee. I won't hear of you offering me money. And I don't want to discuss it anymore."

"It's just that I felt so dreadful after our last parting," Doc said. "I wanted desperately to take you to that dance. I knew how very important it was to you. Unfortunately, my business—"

"Your business is to let bygones be bygones, Doc. The last time you were sweet to me, and if you want to repay me, you can be sweet again."

"For one who has endured persecution for her independence, you still have a magnanimous heart and a forgiving nature, Kathryn."

She stood up and embraced him. Her woman's scent and touch brought out the best in Doc. She was one of the most fascinating women he had ever met. Self-taught, self-styled, and thoroughly baffling.

"I am yours to command for the afternoon," Doc said.

"Then both of us will parade down Main Street arm and arm," Kathryn replied. "I want all of Denver to see that I have a gentleman caller."

"Shall we go?" Doc offered his arm.

"And after our stroll, we will walk by the river and drink wine." Kathryn's face was beaming.

"I shall purchase a fine bottle."

"No need," Kathryn said, putting on her glasses. "I have five gallons of my homemade vintage in the basement."

Doc could not take his eyes off her. "Elderberry, I hope."

"Of course, Mr. Weatherbee, of course."

Her thin coral lips were smiling again. She took Doc's arm,

and they strolled away from the red schoolhouse. Walking with a beautiful woman could do wonders for a man's spirit, Doc thought.

Raider tried to eat his weight in steak and potatoes at the Delmonico Kitchen. When he was full, he strolled in the opposite direction from the schoolhouse. He entered a house on the outskirts of town and asked as to the whereabouts of one Little Bright Wing. A plump woman behind a bar told him that the Indian girl had left to become the wife of a wealthy, older cattleman from Kansas. Raider smiled. He had always hoped the girl would make good.

The woman behind the bar lit a thin stogie. "So, you want to stay anyway?" she asked.

Raider leaned over the bar and smiled at her. "Well, that depends. You got any snatch around here that comes up to Little Bright Wing?"

"Some." She smiled broadly. "How about me?"

"I don't fool around with a woman that smoke cigars. How about giving me a clean room near the bathhouse?"

The cigar-smoking woman laughed and tossed Raider a key. He tromped up a narrow flight of stairs, carrying his rifle on his shoulder. When he opened the door to his room, he saw a young woman lying under the covers. The room smelled like her perfume.

"Is it eight o'clock already?" she asked.

"No, honey," Raider replied. "I'm just sleepin' here. Unless you're feelin' horny?"

"Wanna *sleeep*."

Raider shrugged. "Fine by me. But you're gonna have to keep me warm."

He used a pitcher and bowl to scrub himself clean before he slid under the sheets. The bed was warm. He smelled the woman's blond hair, long and thin, tangled in the pillow. As the bed sagged down, their bodies slid together. Raider felt her warm, moist skin. He started to stroke her shoulder.

She wasn't having any of it. "Wanna *sleeep*, cowboy."

Raider pulled back his hand. "'Scuse me for likin' women."

Reflexively, she rolled over and threw her arm over his

chest. Raider waited until she was dozing again before he guided her hand down to his crotch. He rested her fingers on his semi-erect cock, waiting for her to come back to life. Slowly her fingers started to move up and down the length of his shaft. Her eyes suddenly popped open.

"Son of a bitch," she said. "Looks like a horse done climbed into bed with me."

His prick was growing harder under her touch. She reached down with her other hand, stroking him, throwing back the covers so she could see the prized manhood that swelled in her palms. She laughed a little.

"Damn me if that ain't a hell of a spike, big boy. Looks like I might just have to put that thing inside me."

Raider touched her breast. "What do you think I'm here for?"

She rolled over and straddled his crotch. "Let me guide it along," she said.

"Afraid you can't take it all?"

She laughed. "Wait and see. They don't call me Loose Lucy for nothin', cowboy."

Raider felt the moist lips of her cunt. She grabbed his prick, prodding her vaginal opening. Raider expected her to take it slow, but she engulfed his entire prick with one motion. Her face contorted into an expression of agony. Raider was pretty sure that he wasn't hurting her, however. Her wide hips started moving up and down.

"You filled me up, cowboy," she muttered, kissing his mouth. "You the only one ever done that."

Her body shook and quivered. Raider sucked on her brown nipples. She licked her lips, smiling wickedly.

"Maybe we oughta have you on top, big man."

Raider cupped her buttocks and spun around in one motion, keeping his cock inside her. Lucy raised her legs toward the ceiling. Raider started to move his hips, bouncing her up and down on the soft mattress. He was afraid the floor was going to collapse.

Lucy groaned. "Can't you fuck me any harder?"

"You want it hard and fast, huh? You're gonna git it, then."

Raider tried to drive his cock all the way through her. Lucy shook with each thrust, taking everything he gave her. Raider collapsed on top of her, shoving his cock to the hilt, releasing his milky discharge into her deep cunt. Lucy cried out and dug her fingernails into his ass.

"You fuck good, cowboy. And you've got a hell of a big cock. I want to keep it in there as long as I . . . Hey, what the hell?"

Raider rolled off her. He leaned back, putting his face into the pillow. He snorted and closed his eyes.

"Hey, you all tuckered out?" She nudged his shoulder.

"I just come in off the trail, honey," Raider replied. "I got to get me some shut-eye."

"You can't go to sleep, cowboy. I want some more of that long stuff."

"Leave me be!" Raider pulled the covers over his head.

"Just like a man," she cried. "You dipped your wick and now you want to sleep."

"Out!"

Raider pushed her off the mattress. She hit the floor with a thud. Raider kept one eye open to make sure she wasn't retrieving a weapon from the closet. Lucy wrapped a feathery housecoat around her body.

"I don't need your big cock!" she cried. "I'll go sleep with one of the other girls. We'll do things that you never even thought of."

"I don't care what you do, as long as you leave me alone."

The door slammed. Raider got up and locked it. He had to smile. Whores sure could be fiery once you got them going. He knew the only way to have the bed to himself was to make her mad. And he had gotten laid in the process. Maybe she'd come back after she cooled off.

Raider fell back into the mattress. As he started to drift off, he thought about all the fun a man could have in Denver. If he woke up in time, he planned to take advantage of everything the town had to offer. Not that he wasn't already well along his way.

Doc and Kathryn settled into the tiny stone cottage after dinner. Doc built a warm, flickering fire to stave off the impending chill of night. Kathryn insisted on making tea, but Doc told her he preferred another taste of her homemade wine. They had been drinking it all afternoon, and it seemed a shame to waste the wine's soothing effect on the senses. Kathryn's thin lips broke into a sweet smile.

"You know where I keep my bottles," she said. "Why don't you fetch us another, my dear?"

Doc kissed her cheek and strode toward the "cellar." It was really a small storage area beneath the floor, barely big enough for Kathryn's cache of wine. Doc retrieved a bottle and went back into the tiny parlor.

"Hello, Mr. Weatherbee."

Doc almost dropped the bottle of wine. Kathryn had removed her dress and was lying back on the couch as naked as Eve. Her long legs were spread invitingly. The fire cast fingers of light on her blondish mound of pubic hair. She wasn't ashamed of her nakedness.

"Kathryn, I—"

"Hush," she said. "I don't want you to leave me this time."

Doc was never disappointed when he saw her unclothed. "You're beautiful, Kathryn."

"Put down that wine and take off your clothes, Mr. Weatherbee."

Her nakedness had caught him off guard. But when he looked at her white skin, those budding breasts and pink nipples, when he saw the blond hair streaming behind her, Doc realized that there was no sense in resisting her. Such pretense had no place in the lives of two people who were always perched at the boundaries of the social order.

"Have I offended you?" she asked.

"No, on the contrary," Doc said. "I have offended myself with my own morality. You are being perfectly frank."

She folded her arms over her pert breasts. "Undress and keep me warm."

Doc disrobed and offered his hand. She came to him, pressing her soft skin against his. They stretched out on the floor, the old maid and the detective, warmed by each other and the fire. Doc had never seen her so hungry.

"I want you inside me."

Doc reached between her legs and felt the wetness.

"We have nothing to be ashamed of," she said.

"'Shall I compare thee to a summer's day?'"

He rested his hips between her legs. For an awkward moment he prodded her, trying to enter her tight vagina. Slowly she accepted him, her wet muscles contracting on the length of his penis. Doc kissed her tenderly, working his hips in an easy motion.

"Don't ejaculate inside me," she said. "Please."

"I won't, I promise."

They played lover's games in front of the fire, working themselves into a feverish pitch and then stopping before the moment of culmination. Finally she was too much for him and Doc had to withdraw from her, squirting his viscous discharge all over her stomach. Kathryn laughed and stirred his offering with her slender fingers.

"I love you, Doc."

"I love you too, Kathryn, I only wish that I—"

She put a finger to his lips, urging him to be quiet. "I know what you're going to say. You're going to tell me that you can't love me the way I should be loved. And that I need a husband to treat me like a queen. Well, what if I told you that I don't want to be a queen? What if I told you that I like being an old-maid schoolteacher?"

"Twenty-eight is not old, Kathryn."

"It is if you aren't married. An old maid isn't supposed to have any fun or any rights. She's at the mercy of the community, the fine citizens who frown on a single woman living alone. Well I say fie to those citizens. I'll live my life the way I want to."

"Even without a job?"

She shook her head. "I don't want to think about that, Doc. I want to think about pleasant things."

"But you must face the truth, Kathryn. If you aren't allowed to teach, how will you support yourself?"

"I'm not the religious sort," she replied. "But if you want something badly enough, things have a way of working out. I've done all right so far."

"Kathryn, you are the most spirited person I have ever had the pleasure of knowing." He kissed her hand.

"Oh, stop all this maudlin conversation and pour us two more glasses of wine, Mr. Weatherbee. And put another log on the fire."

Doc got up and did exactly as she said. He was starting to feel rather melancholy as he poured the elderberry wine. Women like Kathryn added a totally different meaning to life. She made a man stop thinking about guns and criminals. Doc suppressed the errant thoughts of what it might be like to have a family.

"Hurry with the wine," she said, "I'm chilly."

"Patience is a virtue, my dear, if you would only . . ."

"What is it, Doc?"

The sight of her sprawled out in front of the fire prompted him to put down the glasses of wine. He was no longer thirsty. Suddenly he had another urge that needed quenching. Kathryn smiled when she saw his erection. She lifted her hand to Doc, inviting him to lie between her legs once more.

Raider awoke to the sound of a rinky-tink piano that was playing below in the parlor of the cathouse. He rose and splashed his face with water. He gazed out toward the busy town, which was lit with the flames of bright gaslights. Denver sure seemed to be alive. And if his memory served him, he knew a few places where a fellow with some money might have a pretty good time.

Raider checked his pants pockets and found two double eagles. Doc had some of his back pay, but it didn't amount to much more than ten or fifteen dollars. Where the hell was Doc, anyway? Raider decided that it didn't matter as he pulled on his boots. He felt something in the toe of his right boot and then remembered Red Claw's Indian charm. Raider shook the pendant out of his boot and strung it around his neck. When his boots were on, he looked for his Stetson until he realized that Red Claw had traded for it.

Raider stomped down the cathouse stairs and tossed one of his gold pieces to the cigar-smoking woman behind the bar.

"Take out what I owe and put the rest to my account."

"Hear you had quite a tumble with Lucy."

"Don't believe everything you hear." Raider pushed out into the street.

As he walked into the heart of Denver, he decided he wasn't

hungry. He looked for a hat shop, to purchase a new Stetson, but all the stores were closed. The double eagle was starting to burn a hole in his pocket. He wondered if the gambling parlor was still in operation. A bell was chiming nine times somewhere in town. Raider turned onto a dim, dirty street and counted doors until he arrived at a white house.

A voice sounded behind a locked door when Raider knocked. "What you want, cowboy?"

"Beulah sent me," Raider replied.

"Haven't heard that one for a while," said the scar-faced man who opened the door. "They ran ole Beulah out of town about two months ago."

Raider smiled at the man. "Hope my money's still good here."

"Come on in, partner, and lose it all."

The faro table was closed, which didn't bother Raider because he wasn't much of a faro player. Blackjack didn't interest him because he could lose twenty dollars pretty fast. The poker table was full. Raider's ears caught the sound of a turning wheel of fortune.

Raider stopped a well-dressed gambler. "Where's the wheel, partner?"

"Back room." The man gestured in the general direction.

Raider had to fight his way through a crowd to get to the wheel. He watched the wooden spokes slowing down as the wheel stopped on number 135. The crowd moaned. Apparently there were no winners. Raider leaned over and looked at the betting table. No one had placed a bet on 135. Almost all of the other two hundred numbers on the wheel had been bet.

"Place your bets," cried the man who worked the wheel. "Put your money down, forty to one pays if you hit."

Raider stood back and watched again. The number came up 113. Again no winner. The wheel was probably fixed, but that didn't matter if you bet on the right number. And both numbers had come up with 13 as part of the combination. That made sense if the wheel was rigged, because people didn't like to bet on 13. They had caught thirteen Bledmans, Raider thought.

A barker hawked the crowd, urging them on. "Get 'em down before the wheel stops movin'. Hurry, hurry."

Raider nonchalantly put the twenty-dollar gold piece on 13. His heart thumped as the wheel slowed: 10, 11, 12 . . .

"Thirteen," cried the barker. "No winners."

Raider stepped up. "Look again, partner. That's my twenty-dollar gold piece."

The crowd stirred.

The barker looked at the double eagle and then at Raider. "You slipped that in on me, cowboy."

A man next to Raider piped up. "He bet it fair and square. I seen him with my own eyes. You better pay up or you're gonna have a riot."

Everyone else echoed the man's sentiment. The barker called for the manager, who listened to Raider and then ordered the barker to pay off—forty to one. Raider had won eight hundred dollars.

The barker shrugged. "Have to pay you in script."

"Any way is fine by me," Raider replied.

"Don't leave before you've had some fun," the manager urged.

Raider spent two hundred dollars at the blackjack table before he tucked away the rest of his winnings and started back to the cathouse. He was halfway down the street when he heard a man's hoarse voice.

"Hold it right there, cowboy. Turn back slow and take that money out of your pocket."

Raider saw him in the shadows, holding a rifle. It was the same old man who had insisted that Raider be payed at the wheel. Raider really didn't feel like killing him. As he reached for the money, he heard the rifle lever squeaking. The old man was jacking a shell into the chamber. Raider pulled his .45 and shot at the old man's hand, hoping to wing him and make him drop the rifle. He missed the man's hand. The old geezer fell into the street with a hole in his chest.

"Son of a bitch." Raider started toward the body.

Suddenly three men were in the street, bending over the dead body of the man who had tried to rob him. One of the men was the manager of the gambling house. He rose from the body and came toward Raider.

"You better clear out, cowboy."

"What about that old man?" Raider asked. "I mean, I didn't want to kill him."

"Of course you didn't," the manager replied. "Now, just go back where you came from."

"What about the law?"

The manager shook his head. "The law is exactly what I don't need, cowboy. If bodies start pilin' up outside my house, they're going to close me down for certain. Now you just get gone. We'll take care of everything."

Raider's gut was stirring. "Hell, I don't like shootin' a man. And over money, at that."

"If it makes you feel any better, this old bastard would have splattered you from here to Sunday for that six hundred dollars."

Raider glared at him. "How'd you know what I'm carryin'?"

The manager clapped him on the back. "I got good eyes. I saw this old bastard leave after you. I waited until the shootin' had stopped before I came out."

Raider kept his eyes on him. "Why'd you wait?"

"Well, if I found you both dead, then I'd get all my money back. Now go, before I change my mind and shoot you myself."

The other two men had already taken the body into the house. Raider turned and hurried back down the street. He wasn't as pleased about the money he had won. It was blood money now. He didn't even feel like springing for a new hat. Bitter-damn-sweet.

When he returned to the cathouse, the cigar-smoking woman laughed at him. "Get into any trouble, cowboy?"

Raider started for the stairs. "My share, lady, my share."

"You got more trouble waitin' upstairs, big boy."

Raider reached down for his gun.

She laughed. "Not that kind of trouble."

"What?"

"Go up and see."

As Raider ascended the stairs, he saw that a line of girls had formed outside his room. Lucy was first in line. The other girls eyed him as he reached for the doorknob.

"What you whores wantin'?" Raider growled.

"They heard about you, cowboy," Lucy said. "And they's all wantin' their turns."

Raider counted six of them.

He shrugged. "Hell, why not? It might settle my nerves. You comin' in first, Lucy?"

The other girls protested that she had already taken her turn. Raider smiled as Lucy told them to shut up. She pushed past him, into his room.

"Don't worry," Raider called to the disappointed girls. "I'll save some for ever'body. Y'all'll get your chance."

He closed the door behind him. Lucy was already lying on the bed, naked. Her legs were spread wide.

"I thought you was goin' to see another girl," Raider quipped.

"Just shut up and take out that big cock of yours," Lucy responded.

"Easy, girl,"

Raider unbuttoned his pants, thinking that it was going to be a long, enjoyable night.

Doc reached the offices of the Medicine Bow Silver Company before Raider. As promised, Hobert Bixley provided Doc with maps and a list of the Medicine Bow employees. Raider came through the office door as Doc was going over the maps of the silver claim. He looked funny without his hat, Doc thought.

Hobert Bixley arrived just as Raider was looking over Doc's shoulder. The old gentleman appeared rested and in good spirits. He gestured to the material in Doc's possession. "Good job, Mr. Weatherbee. I see you wasted no time finding the papers I left here for you. I'm waiting for a scribe to finish the transcription of the reports concerning the, well, the occurrences. It should be ready this morning."

Doc held up a parchment. "Is this map of the mining operation accurate?"

Bixley nodded. "Correct, sir. Three shafts, only one in operation now."

"What is this fourth set of lines?"

"Those lines mark the shaft that collapsed, the one that killed my partner."

"I'd like to see the reports concerning his death."

"As you wish," Bixley replied. "It will take me a few minutes to find the file. If you will be patient."

"Maybe we oughta have some breakfast and come back later," Raider offered. "I got to buy me a new Stetson, too."

Doc nodded and donned his hat. "Come on, Raider. Let's leave Mr. Bixley to his devices. We shall return within the hour, sir. I'd like to leave for the Medicine Bow area before noon."

Bixley agreed that they should leave as soon as possible. With that, Doc and Raider strode out onto the sidewalk. Raider asked Doc for ten dollars to buy a new hat. He didn't feel like spending his gambling winnings. A hat might bring bad luck if it was purchased with blood money.

Doc reached for his wallet. "It's a good thing I held back some of your pay. Otherwise you might be broke."

"If you only knew the truth, Doc."

Raider left Doc to visit the hat shop. He purchased a black Stetson that fit perfectly. He felt good walking down the street with a new hat. He was heading for the Delmonico Kitchen when he saw Doc talking to the pretty blond woman. The woman slapped Doc and turned away crying. She ran toward the ringing school bell at the end of the street.

"What was that all about?" Raider asked.

Doc shrugged him off. "It was nothing."

Raider could see that the blond woman had rattled Doc.

"Maybe you oughta tell me about it, old buddy."

"It's personal." Doc wouldn't look at him.

"She your schoolmarm?"

Doc's face was red as he turned toward his partner.

"Mind your own business, Raider."

Raider bristled. "I thought we was partners. I thought you trusted and respected . . . well, trusted me, anyway."

"There are some matters that are beyond your calloused heart."

"No need to be insultin', Doc. Hell, maybe you oughta wire the office and ask for another partner."

"I'm sorry, Raider. I'm just angry."

"Tell me about it over breakfast."

Doc finally told him about Kathryn's predicament. Raider listened, shoving forkfuls of scrambled eggs into his mouth.

THE GHOST MINE 83

Doc slumped back in his chair, staring into his coffee cup. "I feel so helpless," he finished, shaking his head.

"Hell," Raider replied with a laugh. "I guess things are gonna work out better than you thought."

Raider took out the wad of script money that he had won at the wheel of fortune. Doc's eyes bulged as Raider dropped the cash on the table.

Doc looked at his partner. "Where did you get all of this?"

"I won it fair and square, Doc. I ain't no thief."

Doc glared skeptically at him. "You never give up money unless it's tainted. Did you by any chance kill somebody for this?"

"I won it on a wheel of fortune. Then somebody tried to take it away from me. I had to kill him even though I didn't want to."

Doc smiled and shook his head. "I'm appreciative, but even if I took this money, which I can't . . ."

"Take it or I'm just gonna waste it. Hell, I might not even spend it. Money don't mean that much to me. You know that, Doc."

"Don't you see, Raider, even if I accepted the money, I couldn't get Kathryn to take it. She's too proud."

Raider leaned over the table. "Use your head. Hell, you're sneakier'n a coyote when you want to be."

"You mean trick her into taking the money?"

"Why not? Ain't a woman ever tricked you into giving her some?"

"Raider, your logic usually escapes me, but this time I believe that you're onto something." Doc's eyes had come to life again.

A waitress refilled their coffee cups while the plan stewed.

Doc finally leaned forward. "Let's say that I take this money and have the bank draw up a check. Then I can go to Kathryn and tell her I have a friend in the state government who handles grants for purposes very close to her own predicament."

Raider nodded. "I follow you so far. Keep slingin'."

"Then, before we leave, I draft a letter saying that Kathryn has been accepted for a grant to further her education and thereby continue as a certified teacher. I can put everything in an envelope and direct the postmaster to send the check to her five days after our departure."

"Doc, you can pile it higher and deeper'n anybody I ever knowed."

"Do you think it will work?"

"Sounds foolproof to me."

Doc scooped up the money from the table.

"I owe you a favor, Raider."

The big man was embarrassed. "Aw, forget it. You better get movin' if you want to do all that and get out of here before noon."

"Yes, I'll go to the bank first," Doc said. "And then maybe I can—"

"Git gone!"

Doc looked happy as he left. Raider was glad the money had been put to good use. Maybe Doc's schoolmarm could change that money's luck. He waited for an hour before Doc came back with a smile on his face.

"All set, Raider. Shall we return to Bixley's office and finish our business there?"

Doc said he wanted to stop at the schoolhouse on their way out of town, to say goodbye to Kathryn and to set up their little ruse. Raider imagined the teary farewell, thinking that he could do without the mush. Doc babbled on until they were back in the offices of the Medicine Bow Silver Company. However, when Doc read the reports of the goings-on at the silver mine, he was somber once again.

CHAPTER SIX

The report on the phenomena at the Medicine Bow Silver Company's dig had been dictated by Alva Lutrell, the foreman of the operation. He had spoken his own words to a company scribe. The discourse revealed Lutrell to be a simple, straightforward man.

On the first day of April, I came into the mine in the late afternoon. The men were working as hard as they might, but as soon as they laid eyes on me, they told me of things they had been hearing all day. Strange sounds, like moans and cries, then rumbling and voices saying that they would all die if they stayed in the mine. I thought about it and went on a short inspection of the mine. I saw naught that would make me fear.

As I come back toward the dig, I heard a laughing, high and crazy, and I stopped. But the laughing stopped too, so I come back to the men. They asked me if I had heard the laugh and I said yes. They acted scared, but I then figured that they was playing a April fool joke on me and I didn't think no more about it.

Well, the men had been working pretty hard, so I figured they had a break coming to them, and since it was almost quitting time anyway, I pulled out a flask and passed it around. After we drunk, and nobody had enough to be impaired, we all noticed a strange smell coming down the tunnel. It was a sharp and unnatural stench, like sulphur. Well, it was then that Ernest Short cried out, 'It's the smell of Satan!' But I told him to be quiet and for all of them to get out of the mine.

As they was leaving, I lingered back to see if I could find the source of the horrible smell. It seemed to be rising from the number one hole, but I knowed this to be impossible because that was the collapsed hole where Mr. Lymon Partridge was killed. I still walked that way until I heard the rumbling, like a railroad car on steel track. And then a voice was all around my ears, telling me to run if I wanted to live.

I heeded that voice without thinking much more about it. When I run outside, I seen that all of the other men was down the incline, toward camp. I looked back toward the entrance of the mine and saw two shooting balls of fire, coming up right out of the rock. Behind the fire, on the mountain, I saw dancing lights, like the feet of a hundred spirits doing a jig on the slope. Smoke came out of the entrance to the mine shaft, and I fled from those evil sights with the fear of God in me. I told the men later and asked them to swear that they were not April fooling me. They swore they weren't and said they would not go back to work the claim.

I let a couple of hours pass, and I set to thinking during that time. I am not a schooled man, but I know that sometimes things ain't what they seem. After a few more nips of the bottle, I fortified myself enough to return to the mine shaft. I stayed by the entrance for a long time. I heard voices again and the rumbling of Satan's own hooves. I drew my pistol and took it with me into the shaft.

Strong smells of sulphur came from the bowels of the mine. I followed the path back toward the dig. A strange red light was glowing back there. And the rumblings were louder too. It was then that my faith and strength as a Christian man were tried by God. For I saw, blessed Jesus, a dwarf, a little monster with the face of a snake, hobbling toward me with a bucket in his hand. A demon of Satan, he was. He cried out in a horrible voice that made me wonder if the worst was yet to come.

Satan himself appeared behind the little demon. His head was sprouting horns, and his ugly face appeared that of a wolf. He shot fire from his fingertips and hollered at me in a powerful voice. I ran from him, knowing that my pistol would be no good against the Devil himself. As I came out of the shaft, the arms of fire shot up out of the rock. Ghosts and demons were cackling, dancing on the hillside behind me. Sulphur filled the air as well.

When I came back to camp, I told the men of these things. They went back with me and saw the fire and the ghost lights. We stayed below the mountain, in the trees, all night. When the moon was low on the horizon, we felt the wind shifting to the south. One of the men cried out and pointed into the sky. It was a white eye of Satan, rising into the sky. His eye was burning flame in the center. This was a surprise to all of us, because we had knowed that Satan lives underground. But he rose off to the heavens, and all of the other things stopped.

We waited until the sun was up and then we went into the shaft. Things was normal, except for some of the soot left by Satan and his dwarf. When I took a look at the dig, I saw that Old Pitch had struck a deposit of the purest silver I have ever saw. He had taken out some of the silver, but had left a great deal. I told the men that we would get to work, but they said they were not going to stay in the shaft one minute longer.

Later that morning, Ernest Short came to me and told me that he spoke for the men when he said, 'If Satan wanted that silver, he could damn well have it.' Well, this Short is something of a bully, so I asked the men myself and they said the same. I would work the claim

myself, but after what I have saw I am afeared to go into
the mine alone.

If Satan himself is mining that ore, he has taken out
most of it by now. I'd estimate our losses at fifteen
thousand, maybe more or less. I hearby swear that all
of what I done spoke is true and honest.

Lutrell had signed the statement with a shaking hand. Doc
folded up the parchment and replaced it inside his coat pocket
with the other documents given him by Hobert Bixley. Then
he glanced over at Raider, who still slept beside the smoldering
remains of the fire. They were two days out of Denver, camped
near the rising slopes of the Medicine Bow Mountains. Mists
hung in the forest between the trees, rendering an eerie smoke
in the morning light.

"Roll out, Raider," Doc said. "We'll make the silver claim
by midday if we get moving."

Raider grunted and sat up. He had not even read Lutrell's
statement. Nor would he listen to it in Bixley's office. Doc had
to admit that the story was spooky. As a learned man, however,
he could not allow himself to believe Lutrell's assumption that
the Devil himself was in charge. He did not doubt that the
events had happened, but he was going to assume that everything could be explained by logical deduction.

"You gonna make us some coffee?" Raider rubbed his eyes.

"Why don't we forgo the coffee?" Doc replied. "I'd like to
get moving. I'm eager to investigate the foreman's story."

"Spooks and devils, huh?" Raider muttered. "Hell, I'd wel-
come the chance to go after some murderin' desperado right
now."

"You'll have to read the foreman's statement sooner or later."
Doc held out the report. "Otherwise you will be no help at all
to me."

"Can't you just tell me about it?" Raider groaned.

"Yes, I suppose so."

Raider looked toward the green peaks of Medicine Bow.

"Damn it all, we're back in the woods again, Doc. We ain't
too far from that fishin' hole where Red Claw saved us. Hell,
we're retracin' our own footsteps."

Doc tried to sound convincing. "I wouldn't worry too much."

"I ain't worried."

But Doc could tell by the way Raider watched the shifting mountain mists that he wasn't happy either.

The mists dried up as the sun rose into the sky. A boldly marked trail took them back into the trees, through the low-lying woods, toward the rising slopes of the Medicine Bow junipers. Raider was somewhat relieved when he saw a sign declaring, NO TRESPASSING. MEDICINE BOW SILVER CO. The trail widened, allowing Doc and Raider to ride side by side. Doc had been telling him the story dictated by the foreman.

"What do you think, Raider?"

"I think we better keep our hands close to our guns, Doc."

"You mean you intend to fight the Devil?"

"If I have to," Raider replied.

They followed the road to the wooden structures that appeared above them in a cleared section of forest. A cluster of small brown shacks sat in the lower part of the clearing. Doc took this to be the barracks of the mining crew. Above the barracks rested a house formed out of thick beams and cedar planks. Doc couldn't see the entrance of the mining operation, but he surmised that the path behind the cedar house led up to the mine on the forested slope above.

Raider peered upward. "The big house is probably the minin' office."

"Be careful when we pass the barracks."

They rode slowly past the circle of six men, all of whom were concentrating on something in the center of their group. One of them looked up as Doc and Raider passed by. He alerted the others, who also looked up. Raider saw a woman in the middle of the group. She was dressed like a Gypsy. She also peered at them with black, burning eyes.

Raider shuddered. "I ain't likin' it around here already."

"I thought I saw one of them mouthing the word 'Pinkerton,'" Doc said. "Apparently we've been expected."

"I wonder what they're doin' with that Gypsy woman?"

"No doubt trying to change their luck. I'll bet she's told them she'll chase away the bad spirits for a dollar."

Raider counted six miners. "Small crew."

"That's all they would need for a silver mine," Doc replied.

"You don't have to take out tons of ore to get rich."

"I hear you talkin', Doc. I hear you talkin'."

They stopped in front of the big house, fixing their reins on a wooden hitching post at the bottom of the incline. They ascended a long set of wooden steps, climbing up a slope to the ledge where the office had been built.

Doc rapped on the door and heard a woman's voice bidding him to enter. He looked at Raider. "A woman! I wonder who she is? Be on your best behavior if she's a lady."

"Open the daggone door, Doc."

They found a handsome woman sitting behind a desk. She was younger than thirty, Doc thought, with a clear complexion and the finest auburn hair. When she stood, he saw that she was wearing a rather modest blouse and a long skirt. Raider noticed the impressions of her red nipples under the tight fabric of the cream-colored blouse. Her voice was clear and confident.

"Are you the Pinkertons?"

Doc nodded and showed her their credentials.

"We're here to see Lutrell," Raider said. "Mr. Bixley sent us. If we could..."

Tears pooled in her brown eyes. She put her face in her hands and sat down, sobbing. Doc shook his head.

"You've made her cry, Raider."

"I didn't do nothin'."

Doc tried to console her. "I'm sorry if my partner upset you. He can't help himself sometimes."

"No," she said. "Your partner didn't. It's Mr. Lutrell. He's dead."

Doc was taken aback.

"Yesterday," the woman sobbed. "We found him up near the mine. His body is on the back porch. I've tried, but I can't get any of the miners to bury him. They say the Devil took his soul and that they'll lose their souls if they give him a Christian burial."

Doc offered her his handkerchief. "Calm yourself, Miss..."

"Bixley," she replied. "Diandra Bixley."

Raider took off his Stetson. "You any relation to Hobert Bixley?"

"He's my father." She blew her nose.

"He didn't tell us you were going to be here," Doc said.

"He doesn't know. I've been in San Francisco for the past two years. He thinks I'm still there."

"Why did you come here?" Raider asked.

"My mother wrote me that there was trouble up here at the mine. I came on my own to see if I could help. You see, I was engaged to be married, but unfortunately it did not . . . well, I was never wed. I've been in business school for a year, so I had hoped that I could be of some assistance here."

Raider hated to see her crying with such a pretty face. "Don't worry, we're gonna help you."

"Why didn't you tell him you were coming here?" Doc asked.

"He wouldn't approve of his daughter trying to help his business."

"Are you aware of the bizarre reports concerning the occurrences at the mine?"

"I've seen the fire coming out of the rocks," Diandra replied. "Alva Lutrell took me up there before he . . ."

She started to cry again. Doc patted her shoulder, and she threw her arms around him. Raider shook his head. High-class women always went for Doc's fancy manners. A cowboy wouldn't have a chance with a woman like Diandra Bixley.

Doc was right there by her side. "Excuse me, Diandra, but if I may, I would like to see Mr. Lutrell's body."

"Certainly," she replied. "It's on the back porch."

"Thank you." Doc started away.

"Mr. Weatherbee."

"Yes."

"You may not want to look at the body. Supposedly, he was . . ."

"Go on, Miss Bixley."

"Supposedly, he was clawed to death by Satan."

Miss Bixley followed them to the back porch. The corpse was lying on a table. A canvas shroud covered the remains of Alva Lutrell. Doc was rather sorry that he was never going to meet Mr. Lutrell. From his statement, Doc had pictured him as a good man. He rolled back the canvas and examined the corpse.

"I never looked," Diandra said to Raider.

"Can't say as I blame you," Raider replied.

She was standing too close to him. Her perfume almost took his mind off the dead body. He hoped Doc wouldn't ask him to look. If Doc asked, Raider would have to oblige him. He didn't want Diandra Bixley to know he was afraid to gaze on the corpse.

"Something got to him," Doc said. "Long, thin claw marks. Raider, would you take a look?"

Raider held his breath and peered over Doc's shoulder. The sight wasn't as bad as he had figured. He had once seen a man who had been attacked by a mountain lion. He sure as hell hadn't looked as good as Alva Lutrell.

Raider shook his head. "He wasn't clawed by no mountain lion."

Doc nodded. "I concur. I'd say those marks were made with metal tines. And look, there in the chest. Blood encrusted under his shirt. This man was shot first and then mangled to make it look like a horrendous slaying."

A scream rose up from below the house. The shrill, banshee howling resounded through the trees and back into the pits and crevices of the mountain.

Diandra Bixley put her hand to her mouth. "What now?" she cried.

Apparently the Gypsy woman had screamed, but when Doc and Raider rushed onto the front steps, they saw she was not in danger. Instead, she stood behind the group of men that had gathered at the bottom of the steps. A grizzled, portly man stood in front of the group. From Lutrell's report, Doc figured the man to be Ernest Short.

"We come to see the woman," Short said.

"I'm afraid you will deal with us at this point " Doc replied. "We are here to investigate the goings-on in this area. Your cooperation and the cooperation of these men—"

Short broke in. "They's my men now, dandy. They's voted me foreman. We want our back pay and then we're clearin' out."

Doc forced a smile. "Sir, you must be patient in this matter."

"You lookin' to git your back busted, Mr. Pinkerton?"

"If you persist with this attitude, you will be the one to get hurt, Mr. Short."

He eyed Doc with a sidelong glance. "How'd you know my name, dandy?"

"He knows shit that would turn you inside out," Raider barked. "So you just take your men and run along. If you got back pay comin', we'll see that you get it."

"Your ape always do the talkin' for you, dandy?" Short said.

"Anytime you're wantin' to try me, Short."

"Raider!"

"Hell, Doc, it might be the best way to deal with this boy," Raider growled. "Just stand toe to toe with him before he causes any trouble."

Doc shook his head. "We don't want to stir up anything that might make things worse. Mr. Short, how much back pay do you have coming?"

Short was wary. "Three weeks. That's what we all have coming."

"Very well. I can assure you that you will receive all of your back wages. However, I would like to pose one question. How many of you here would like to have your jobs back? Raise your hands. Don't be afraid of Mr. Short here."

All the men raised their hands.

Short was still riled. "Who wouldn't want their job back? But I'm tellin' you, the Devil's livin' up there on that mountain. He don't want none of us comin' up there."

"Give me one week, gentlemen," Doc said. "If I do not have a solution to our problem, then you will get one month's back pay. You have my word as a gentleman and a Pinkerton."

They mulled it over. The majority wanted to give Doc a chance. Only Short was reluctant.

Finally he looked up at Doc. "One week," Short said. "No more."

The miners moved away, back toward their shacks. The Gypsy woman stepped aside to let them pass. She had caught Raider's eye. Quickly she met his gaze and smiled. Raider looked away.

Doc hooked his thumbs in his vest pocket. "We must keep an eye on Short."

"You should have let us go at it with fists," Raider replied. "A bully backs down when you call his bluff."

"Stay ready," Doc said. "You never know when you're going to get an opportunity to match him."

Diandra Bixley came out behind them.

"Is everything all right?" she asked.

Doc nodded reassuringly. "Tell me, is there a stable hereabouts? We need to take care of our animals."

She pointed down the slope. "Can you see it? There's a corral down there. I suggest you leave your wagon here, where you can keep an eye on it."

"I concur," Doc replied. "Raider, will you take the animals down to the corral?"

"What are you plannin' on doin'?"

"I'm going to stay here and talk to Miss Bixley."

"That's what I thought," Raider mumbled. "Boy, them ladies really get him goin'. He'll be sirin' and missin' and mammin' the whole cotton-pickin'—"

"I beg your pardon, Raider?"

"Never mind, Doc. Never mind."

Raider unsaddled his gray and threw the tack into the rear of Doc's wagon. Then he released Judith from her harness and led her down the incline with the gray. The corral had been fashioned intelligently, Raider thought. A circle had been cut in the forest and then barbed wire had been strung around the tree trunks along the perimeter of the circle. Logs were placed diagonally against the wire to keep the animals from bumping into the sharp barbs. Raider put Judith and the gray into the corral and forked over hay from the haystack. When he turned back toward the house, he saw Short and the other men standing behind him.

"Well, Pinkerton," Short said. "Looks like you're down here with the rest of us."

Short was holding a Colt pocket revolver. Raider's hand hung loosely by his side. None of the other men were carrying guns. If Raider could take Short before he got off a shot, he'd be able to stare down the other men. But if Short got lucky...

Raider squared his shoulders. "You ain't gonna pull on me, Short."

"How you know that? Maybe you got it comin' to you. Ridin' in here to take over ever'thing. That girl up yonder don't know what she's doin'."

"I know you ain't gonna muster the backbone. And even if you do, my partner up there will come after you. And if he don't get you, then there'll be other Pinkertons. We take care of our own. Besides, if you shoot me, I might take all six rounds and still put one right between your eyes. So, you want to try?"

Short was afraid in front of his men. "You lookin' to git your back busted, Pinkerton?"

Raider smiled. "You can try. Unless you're yellow."

"No man calls me yellow!"

Raider held up his fists. "If you feel froggy, then how about jumpin'?"

Short tossed the pistol to the ground. Raider unbuckled his holster and hung it on the gate of the corral. He turned back to see Short rushing him. Short's fists were flying at his head. Raider ducked and let him run into the corral. Short cried out as he stuck himself on the barbed wire.

Raider backed away and laughed. "Had enough, Short?"

Short stalked him again, slower this time. Raider crouched into a fighting posture with his fists up. When Short tried to hit him, Raider swung low into his stomach and ribs. He felt cartilage breaking under his fist. Short grunted and staggered backward holding his gut. Raider thought he might be finished.

"Give it up, Short. You don't want to—"

Short came at him again. His ugly face was contorted in a hideous rage. Raider sidestepped him and brought down his fist on the back of Short's neck. Short stumbled forward, landing on his face in a pile of manure.

"Looks like you found what the horse left behind," Raider chuckled.

Short came up looking for his gun. "I'm gonna shoot this bastard."

His pocket revolver was lying a few feet away. Raider measured the distance to his .45. Short crawled after his weapon. Raider dived for his holster and came up with the Colt's hammer cocked. Short was looking up at a small man who had his foot on the pocket revolver.

"If you can't take him fair," said the small man, "then don't try to take him at all."

Raider slipped his .45 back into the holster.

"Come on, Short. Show your men what you're really made of."

The ugly man came up again, charging like a bull. Raider tried the side move again, but Short was on to him. He caught Raider's leg and drove him back into the haystack. Raider sprawled backward, bumping his head on a tree. Short picked up the hayfork and lifted it to impale Raider. A shotgun blast kept him from finishing the job. Buckshot kicked up the ground next to Short's feet.

"That will be enough out of you," cried Diandra Bixley.

She was standing there with a Remington scattergun that issued smoke from one barrel. Short dropped the fork. The other men backed away. Raider sat up on the haystack and looked at the pretty lady with her hands full.

Short pointed at Raider. "He started it."

"I doubt that," she replied.

Short started toward her.

"I've got another barrel if you want to taste it," Diandra said.

Short advanced no farther. Diandra reached into the folds of her dress and withdrew a leather pouch. She tossed the pouch at Short's feet.

"You're fired, Mr. Short. Here are your back wages."

"You can't fire me," he cried. Then to the other men: "I'm the foreman. You hear me? Tell her. Tell her I'm the foreman."

"You better be gone in the next five seconds," Diandra said.

Short tried another appeal to the men, but they seemed to side with Diandra. The little man who had put his foot on the pistol looked relieved that their new foreman was leaving. Short picked up his money and glared at Diandra. She glared right back.

Short wiped blood from his lip. "You're gonna regret this. You hear? You'll pay more than you already have."

She gestured toward the corral with the shotgun. "Just take your horse and go."

They all watched as Short stormed toward the corral. He rode out bareback on a white mare. Raider had to close the gate to keep the other animals from escaping. Diandra came down to help him with the latch.

"I s'pose I should thank you for helping out," Raider said bashfully. "I guess I kinda have to admire a woman who knows how to use a shotgun."

"Are you all right?" she seemed genuinely concerned.

Raider nodded. "I'll live. I've been busted up worse."

"Miss Bixley," cried the small man. "What you want us to do?"

"Would you return to the house and help Mr. Weatherbee bury the body of Mr. Lutrell." She waited to see if they would obey her.

The men spoke among themselves for a moment. "Yes, ma'am," replied the little man at last. They moved back toward the house.

Raider looked at his battered fist. "They act like they're glad that Short's gone."

"I've been wanting to fire him since I came here. I just didn't have the courage until you arrived. Are you sure you're all right?"

She was standing so close to him, looking up into his eyes. Raider held her shoulders and pressed his mouth to hers. For a moment she kissed him, and then she went as limp as a dishcloth.

Raider pushed her away. "I guess you're thinkin' you're too good for a cowboy like me. I shouldn't have kissed you."

She spoke softly. "No, you shouldn't have kissed me. But let's not make more of this than we have to. Things haven't been as—"

He kissed her again, but she didn't respond.

"You don't like it?"

"I didn't say that, Raider."

She seemed sort of feverish, like he might be getting to her.

"You're so doggone pretty. I couldn't help myself."

"Don't treat me like a common whore."

He was confused. "Damn it, that ain't what I mean. I ain't like Doc. I can't put things into words. When I see a woman like you, I—"

"Please," she said. "Don't say things you don't mean. I suggest we return to the house. Your partner..."

"Yeah, I figured he would come up. Aw hell, I give up. I won't say nothing if you won't."

Raider stormed up the hill, unaware of the gleam in Diandra Bixley's eyes. Her legs were weak and her head was spinning. Raider's desire had too quickly turned to anger.

CHAPTER SEVEN

When Alva Lutrell was underground, Doc invited the miners to sit with him on the back porch, offering a drink of fine Irish whiskey as inducement. With Short gone—how could Doc blame Raider if Short had attacked him?—the men seemed more relaxed. Doc wanted to establish good relations with the mining crew. He would need their cooperation.

"To your continued employment, gentlemen," Doc said, lifting a shot of rye. "Cheers."

"To the memory of Alva Lutrell," said the little man whose foot had kept Short from his pistol.

Doc regarded the elfish gentleman. "And who are you, sir?"

He looked Doc squarely in the eye. "Name's Delp. Tiny Delp. Been hired on here since Hobert Bixley and Lymon Partridge sunk their first pick in that mountain."

Doc thought he looked like a leprechaun. His pointed ears stuck out from under the narrow brim of an old green derby. Salt-and-pepper whiskers sprouted from his thin dry face. A joker's mouth and steely gray eyes.

Delp pointed a crooked finger at Raider. "This 'un had Short whipped," he said. "Then Short tried to cheat. I never took to him much. Glad he's gone."

Raider exhaled. "You saved my bacon, Tiny. Why, if you hadn't stepped on that pistol when you did, I might be up yonder with the other foreman."

"Who's gonna be the new foreman?" Delp asked quickly.

"We'll have to wait for Miss Diandra to say," Raider replied.

"What must I say?" Diandra stood at the back door.

"Mr. Delp here wants you to name a new foreman," Doc said.

Diandra moved toward them in the afternoon shadows. She had a tray of sandwiches for them. The mining crew ate heartily. Diandra ignored Raider as she sat down next to Doc.

"I'll name a foreman when we begin to work the mines again," she replied. "Until then, I am in charge of the office and Doc is in charge of the investigation. I only ask that you do not tell my father I am here until we uncover something."

Doc nodded. "That's agreeable."

Doc turned toward Tiny Delp, who was pushing a piece of bread into his mouth. He chewed and washed it down with whiskey. Every mining operation needed a man like Tiny, a mouse who was able to go anywhere. He could squeeze into crevices and holes that would easily stop a normal-sized man.

Doc smiled. "Mr. Delp, you say you've been here in this area for several years. I was wondering if you had any insights into the strange occurrences of late."

Delp's eyes narrowed. "I weren't lyin' when I said I been here awhile. I come to Medicine Bow more'n thirty years back. That was before the war, when we had trappers and prospectors. I used to work over to the general store by Kiowa Pass. When the war come, I stayed on. Met up with Bixley and Partridge back then. They was younger and lookin' for silver. I think they mighta found it back then, but the war was goin', and when they went back home they was mustered into the Colorado volunteers."

Diandra frowned. "My father never told me that."

"They come back after the claim when the war was over," Delp replied. "By then the general store was closed up, so I went to work for them. Worked for free until they struck it."

"Is it a good strike?" Doc asked.

Delp grinned. "This is the best I ever seen. We're on our fourth tunnel. It just keeps comin', one deposit after another."

"If it's so all-fired rich, why don't you have more guards on up here?" Raider sounded his usual cynical note.

"We employed three security men," Diandra replied curtly. "They left when everything began up there." She pointed toward the mountain.

A cool wind was blowing in from the south, rustling the branches of the forest. An orange pallor spilled down the slope from the west, casting vague shadows between the tree trunks. For a moment, they were all silent. A low, haunting sound rolled out of the valley depths. It was laughter.

"What the hell?" Raider cried, coming up with his .45 in hand.

"It's just that Gypsy woman," Delp said. "She's been tryin' to spook ever'one so they'll give her some money to drive off the spirits."

"Are you sure?" Raider was reluctant to holster the Colt.

"It's too early for anythin' else."

Doc stared at the little man. "What do you mean by too early?"

Delp looked at Miss Diandra Bixley. "I ain't sure I can tell you in front of the lady."

"I assure you, Tiny, I will not be offended by anything you say," Diandra said. "In fact, I would ask you to be totally honest. Hold back nothing that might help Doc and . . . his partner."

Raider felt a sting in his heart. If she was going to play rough, then he would oblige her. "Give us all the gory details, Tiny."

Delp tilted back his hat. His joker face seemed to be smiling. He liked being the center of attention.

"It's a old tale I heard from the first year I was in this territory," he started. "I mean *state,* now. Anyways, story goes like this. Seems there was a trapper's wife livin' up to Ridge Creek. She was a young 'un, a half-breed. Didn't nobody bother her and her husband none. But it goes that the squaw was lonely 'cause her husband was gone all the time, what with his trappin' and all. And this is where it starts to get—"

"Would you like another whiskey?" Doc offered the bottle.

Delp waved him off. "After. See, legend says that two Kiowa bucks was huntin' one day when they spied the trapper's wife in the creek, bathin'. They was young and had their sap up. They commenced tryin' to have their way with her. Only she was wilder'n they figured and they ended up spendin' a couple of nights with her. Trapper came home and killed her and the two bucks. Then he put a torch to the lodge and ran off up in the high country to go crazy. I reckon I mighta done the same."

Raider scoffed. "How you know all this?"

"Like I said, been hearin' that story a long time."

"And you think this incident has something to do with the present situation at the mine?" Doc asked.

"I ain't sayin' either way," Delp replied. "I just know this: that squaw was killed nigh on to fifty years back. Ever since that time, there's been talk of lights on the mountain and sounds that come from Hell. 'Bout once a year, somebody crawls out of the woods to say he's seen spooks and spirits hereabouts. And once in a while somebody goes out on a grubstake and never comes back. Old Mose Clark was the last one I knowed of. Some say the Indian girl lives with the Devil now. They say she tempts men into her lodge and then takes their souls."

"Have you ever talked to anyone who has seen this woman?" Doc asked.

"No, can't say as I have. But I knowed two or three boys who saw the ghost light."

Raider offered a derisive laugh. "I only believe what I can see, and then only half of that."

Delp leaned over, staring straight into Raider's black eyes. "I seen the Devil's own eye flyin' above the mountain. I seen fire out of rock and spooks dancin' on the slopes. I saw the smoke and heard the voice of Lucifer. I smelled his sulphur in the air."

The shadows were creeping in on them. Mists formed in the lower areas of the forest, where the warm wind could not stir them.

Tiny Delp looked up into the mountains and then back at

Doc. "They say a warm south wind wakes her up," he said. "When it blows, you can see the ghost light on dark nights. She's only calm again when the wind blows down from the north. I'll take some more of that whiskey, sir."

Doc poured another round for everyone. He leaned back and gazed up at the twilight slopes. Raider was still holding his .45.

Doc's voice pierced the dusky silence. "I want to take a few precautions to protect ourselves. We must work together. Since Mr. Alva Lutrell was killed, there is reason to believe that whatever killed him might strike again. I want all of you to sleep up here, in the house. I want one of you to be with Miss Bixley at all times when we are not here. Report anything that you hear or see. Do not, I repeat, do not act on your own initiative unless your life is endangered. Is that understood?"

All of them nodded. Diandra Bixley shuddered and pulled a sweater around her shoulders. Raider wondered if he had really kissed her.

"We goin' up on the mountain tonight, Doc?" Raider asked.

Doc shook his head. "I will watch from here tonight, with my glass. If I see anything unusual, we will investigate. Until that time, I suggest that everyone try to get comfortable."

"Me and the boys will sleep in the loft upstairs," Delp said.

"Is that satisfactory, Diandra?" Doc asked.

Diandra smiled and nodded. "I'll have to find some extra blankets. If one of you would be so kind as to accompany me into the house. I won't feel like being alone until I light several lamps. It's going to be dark soon."

"It's dark enough for me right now," Raider offered. "I'll go with you, Diandra."

She stared blankly at the big man from Arkansas. "Very well, let's go."

Raider followed her around while she went through the house lighting six or seven hurricane lamps. She wouldn't look at him, but she kept brushing against his body, finding ways to accidentally touch his hand.

Raider looked down at her as she piled blankets on his arms. "What kind of wheel you spinnin', lady?"

"I don't know what you mean." Her face was blushed-red.

"You put me off at the corral but then you don't say nothin' when I invite myself along. I don't understand this stuff. I guess I'm just a cowboy."

Her face was so innocent as she met his black eyes. She was scared. Raider felt weak inside. He was sort of scared too. Scared of what she was doing to him.

She looked up at him with mysterious eyes. "I was engaged to a swaggering man like you. He left me."

"So all men are bastards?"

"I know of one," she replied coldly. "And I have a strong suspicion about you. If you—"

Raider threw down the blankets and took her into his arms. Diandra let him kiss her for another moment before she turned away.

Raider felt helpless again. He released her from his embrace. "I don't take nothin' that ain't offered freely," he said.

"If I've given you the wrong impression . . ."

He started for the steps.

"Where are you going?"

"To Doc's wagon. I'm tired of foolin' with you. I'm gonna see if Doc has some more whiskey."

"Are you going to leave me alone?" She put a petite hand to her throat.

"You was alone before we got here, lady. Aw, don't worry, I'll send in one of the other boys. Until then, the ghosts will just have to take their chances."

He left her in the dim confines of the loft and found his way downstairs. With a hurricane lamp in hand, Raider strode out of the house, clomping down the long wooden steps to Doc's wagon. He was fishing for a bottle of red-eye when he heard a rustling behind him. Quickly hs spun around, bringing up his .45 into the face of laughter. Female laughter.

"You can't kill me, cowboy," said the Gypsy.

"You better clear the hell out of here, woman."

She laughed in his face. "What have you got there?"

She moved forward into the circle of light that radiated from the hurricane lamp. Raider noticed her breasts immediately. The brown nipples were rigid under her tight white blouse. She looked younger up close. Black hair spilled over her bare shoulders. Raider uncorked the bottle of rye and took a long drink.

Her slender fingers reached for the bottle. "Save some for me."

Raider laughed and handed her the bottle, expecting her to gag on the rotgut that Doc often used for liniment. But she turned up the bottle and took a healthy swig. She wiped her thick lips and gave the liquor back to Raider.

"What do they call you, Gypsy woman?"

"Medea," she replied. "Medea Barnado. I have been summoned here for a great battle between two unearthly forces."

"Summoned by who?"

"By fate," she replied. "Fortune's wheel. She swings up and down."

"Yeah, I know about that shit." She was starting to make him nervous.

Her palm caressed his face. "Don't be vulgar, cowboy. A man as handsome as you should not be vulgar."

Raider laughed. "This whiskey must be gettin' to me. You ain't lookin' so bad yourself, Meddie."

"Medea!"

"Well, I don't give two hoots what you're called, lady. I just know that a woman ain't got much of a chance out here in the wilds by herself."

"Diandra Bixley is alone," she offered coyly.

Raider frowned. "Leave her out of this."

Medea moved closer to Raider. She ran her hands over his chest. Her hair smelled like flowers, he thought. Her lips brushed his neck while her hand started to roam over his crotch.

"I will tell your fortune afterward," she whispered.

"After what?"

"After we make the two-backed beast."

"Is that the same as fuckin'?"

"Come to my camp, cowboy," she whispered. "I will not hurt you. You need a woman like me to do all the things Miss Bixley won't do."

He surrendered. "All right, but if you try any monkey business, I'll shoot you as quick as I would any man."

She just laughed, taking his hands and leading him into the trees with only the hurricane lamp to light their way.

• • •

Doc sat on the back porch, flanked by Diandra Bixley and
Tiny Delp. He sipped tea instead of whiskey. His eyes were
turned upward, toward the star-strewn sky. He thought of Satan
in *Paradise Lost,* leaving a trail of celestial sparks as he started
over the Lake of Fire toward Earth, on his way to tempt Adam
and Eve. There was no moon, but the stars seemed bright
enough to light the way of any night traveler—including demons from Hell.

"Are the other men settled in?" Doc asked.

"Yes, sir," Delp replied. "We're gonna sleep in shifts. That
way we can make sure Miss Bixley is guarded all the time."

"Well done. Have you seen my partner?"

"He went down to your wagon about half an hour ago,"
Diandra said. "How did you ever come to work with such a
rough, ignorant man, Mr. Weatherbee?"

"Has he done something to upset you, Diandra?"

She sat up straight. "No! It's just that . . . that kind of man
infuriates me. I don't wish to speak of him any further."

She was protesting too much, Doc thought. He found it hard
to believe, but she was actually sweet on Raider. Doc was
studying her as wild cries of passion echoed through the forest.
Diandra sat up and looked out into the darkness. Tiny Delp sat
up too.

"It's just that Gypsy woman," Delp said.

Diandra listened intently. "I hope no one is hurting her."

Delp laughed. "He ain't hurtin'—"

Doc jumped in. "Think nothing of it. She's only trying to
stir up the cauldron and somehow realize a profit for herself."

Diandra rose hastily and hurried into the house. She knew
what Raider was doing. It was only natural, Doc thought. If
his partner got near a woman and a bottle of whiskey, sparks
usually flew for a while. Doc just hoped that Raider wouldn't
take all night with his recreation. The big man from Arkansas
would have to stand his watch like everyone else. Doc raised
the spyglass to his eye and gazed into the dark heavens, searching for anything that might be out of the ordinary.

As the Gypsy woman led him down the trail, Raider thought
he might be making a mistake by visiting her camp. But he

stayed behind her, keeping his eyes open, drawn on by the scent of her body. She had a wagon—a cart, really—parked in a small clearing. A burro brayed somewhere in the dark. Medea let go of Raider's hand and bent down to the ground.

"What are you doin'?" Raider asked.

She didn't reply. Her hands worked until a circle of flame rose off the ground. She looked up at Raider and smiled.

"To keep us warm," she said, pulling her blouse off her shoulders.

"I'm feelin' kinda warm already."

He sat the hurricane lamp on the cart. A breeze disturbed the flames of the fire on the ground. Medea's face seemed to flicker in the shadowy fingers of orange reflection. Raider couldn't take his eyes off her nipples. He thought he heard bells on the wind.

Raider sat up. "What the hell is that noise?"

"Only chimes. I strung them in the trees to keep away the bad spirits."

She had begun to spread out a quilt on the ground. Raider raised the bottle to his lips, but he suddenly didn't feel like drinking. Medea knelt on the quilt and looked up at him with her large, brown eyes. Raider offered her the bottle.

She grabbed his hand. "Drink from breasts. You will find them sweet."

"Listen, maybe I oughta go back up to the ..."

His second thoughts were quickly erased by the sight of her jiggling breasts. The nipples were large and firm and brown in the dim glow of the campfire. Raider joined her on the quilt, taking her breasts into his hands, kissing her nipples. She grabbed his face and pressed her mouth to his. Her tongue tasted like whiskey.

She pulled away quickly. "Wait, cowboy, you must eat."

She had taken something from the folds of her black skirt. Slender fingers tried to shove something in his mouth.

Raider grabber her wrist. "What the hell is this?"

"Magic," she replied. "If you don't eat, you don't get me."

"Hell, give it here."

Raider chewed something that was tough and sweet. He figured she wouldn't poison him, what with Doc so close by. He had done stranger things to get a woman.

"Now, come here, lady."

They wrestled on the quilt, kissing and groping. Raider ran his hands over her stomach and her thick thighs. Her breath was wild, like a filly who was ready to accept a stallion. She rolled over on top of him, letting her hair spill down onto his face. Raider gazed up at her in the eerie firelight. Her eyes seemed to be spinning.

Raider was confused. "What the hell is goin' on? What are you doin' to me?"

"Be quiet and let me have you. Don't fight me."

Her hands were all over him, undoing every one of his buttons and buckles. He heard his holster hitting the ground but he didn't care. He was naked by the fire, looking up at the Gypsy woman as she stripped. Her thick body had a good shape, he thought. She straddled his thighs, lowering her broad hips.

"I'm wet," she whispered. "Feel my river."

She rubbed her coarse bush of pubic hair over the expanding length of Raider's cock. He worked his hips, trying to penetrate the slippery folds of her cunt.

Medea lowered her breasts into his face. "Do you feel it?" she asked.

"My head is spinnin'."

"Don't fight, just love, handsome, love. When we are through, I will know everything about you."

Raider felt as if all his strength had left him. He was aware of Medea's cunt, but he couldn't get on top to put it inside her.

She grabbed his cock and rested it against the entrance of her vagina. "You want?" she teased.

"I want."

Her cunt sucked in about half of his cock. Medea grunted and groaned. Raider's eyes would not focus as she worked on him. He was only aware of her voice, directing him, making him do her bidding. Raider could only obey, following her lead like a dutiful slave.

"Rarely do I find a man with powers like yours, my loved one. Get on top of me and give me your power, cowboy."

Raider broke out in a sweat as he settled between her thighs. She was writhing underneath him, her face contorted in the firelight. Raider's body worked without his mind, responding on its own to her vigorous movements. Raider slammed his cock inside her, but he wasn't sure he was screwing her. He seemed to be aware of watching himself performing an arduous ritual. Medea's voice brought him back into his body.

"Don't leave me," she pleaded. "Not as long as you have that long, hard thing between your legs. I want it every way. I want..."

She wrapped her legs around his waist, trapping his cock inside her for a few heated moments. Perspiration poured out of Raider's feverish skin. He collapsed into Medea's bosom, waiting for her next command.

"Get behind me, cowboy."

Raider maneuvered his body to accommodate her. She grabbed his cock and guided it into the pit of her bushy cunt. He obliged her desire, shoving his prick in and out, rocking her body, shaking her fleshy bosom. She cried out so loudly that Raider was afraid that the whole territory might hear her. Medea's ass shook with each thrust of his hips.

"Damn you, big-pricked cowboy...I love that hairy little man between your legs."

Raider didn't have much restraint. He felt his cock expanding. A burst of warm liquid left his body with an involuntary release. He fell forward, pinning the Gypsy woman to the quilt. She didn't protest his weight.

Raider thought he would be limp after his discharge, but his cock remained stiff. Medea squirmed under him until she was once again looking up into his eyes. She was sweating too. Her hand guided him into her cunt.

"Feel the forces of nature," she said, her eyes sparkling. "Feel how you give it to me again."

His body started to work once more. Medea kept him between her legs, summoning energies he had never known. He had just started to hump her when a second release made him tremble. Medea laughed, biting his neck, wiggling beneath his hulking frame.

"I will always think of you when I am with other men," she said. "For the rest of my life. I'd love to cut off your prick and keep it in a bottle."

Raider climbed off her and stretched out next to the fire. He stared up at the boughs overhead. The wind was stirring the trees. He felt like he might be able to top Medea again if she would let him rest for a few minutes.

"What the hell did you give me to eat?"

"A mushroom," she replied. "How do you feel?"

"Like a . . . like a god."

"Shh, do not be blasphemous. Here, let me have your hand. I can read your palm. I will tell you everything that will happen to you."

Raider did not resist as she took his hand.

She sucked in air through her thick lips. "You are a very powerful man. You are in danger, though. I see a dark man, like Satan. I see lights and fire. You will fly, cowboy. You will fly on the wings of a dark angel. You will fall, too, from the sky, like a dead bird."

Raider listened to her, drifting in his head, unable to take her seriously. Her voice lulled him, like the Pacific Ocean, where he had once been with Doc. And Doc's voice came in behind Medea's, calling from that distant place where the blood had pooled in the sand.

"Cowboy! Cowboy, wake up!"

Medea was nudging him. He had fallen asleep by the fire. He sat up and shook his head. His eyes focused on the embers of the campfire. Medea had slipped on her blouse. She threw his clothes at him.

"Somebody's calling you," Medea said.

"How long I been out?"

"About an hour. They started calling for you just now."

Doc's voice came through the night, echoing faintly in the trees. Raider called back as he slipped on his pants. He wondered if Doc would be able to hear him with the wind.

"Damn you, woman. Where's my boots? And my gun?"

"There, by the fire. Here, let me turn up the wick on this lamp."

"Never shoulda come down here anyway." He pulled on a boot.

"Admit it, cowboy, I'm the best you ever had."

"I ain't got time to jerk around," Raider grunted. "Give me that lamp."

She put her hand on his forearm to stop him.

"Let go of me, you female wildcat!"

Her voice was fraught with fear. "Be careful. If you do not heed the warnings of the fates, you will find your death."

Raider pushed her away. "Bullshit. You better stay out of my way, woman. I don't want you gettin' caught in the cross-fire."

Doc's voice urged him up the path. Raider hurried, leaving Medea behind him. What the hell had gotten into him back there? he wondered. She had done funny things to his head. He seemed all right now, though. When he came out of the trees, he saw Doc ahead of him, holding a torch.

"You look like a lost sodbuster, Doc."

"This is no time for jocularity, Raider."

"What the hell is wrong with you?"

Doc's face was flushed. He held an Old Virginia cheroot in his trembling fingers. Raider had never seen him so flustered. He was scared!

"What's goin' on, Doc?"

"I think we'd better move, Raider. I'll tell you why on the way up to the mine."

"The mine? Why the hell are we going up there?"

Doc's face didn't look normal. "I saw something in the sky."

"What?"

"I can't be sure."

"What the hell did you see, Doc?"

"The eye of Satan," Doc replied. "The eye of Satan."

CHAPTER EIGHT

Doc and Raider stood at the base of the dark path, gazing up into the trees. Doc held a torch in his left hand. They couldn't see the entrance to the silver mine from their vantage point. Doc motioned for Raider to follow him up the path.

"I ain't goin' up there till you tell me what you really saw," Raider said.

"Raider, we're wasting time."

"And we're gonna waste a lot more if you don't hurry up and tell me what you saw." Raider stood his ground.

"I'm not exactly sure what I saw."

"Then try to put it in the best words you can. If it's one thing you're good at, it's talkin'."

Doc paused to compose his thoughts. "I was sitting back there on the porch, watching the sky. Diandra and Mr. Delp had gone into the house shortly before it appeared over the peak of the mountain."

"*It?*" Raider didn't like the sound of that.

"A large, dark shape in the sky," Doc said. "Then there was a light. And then . . . and then it sank behind the mountain."

"Hell, if it's on the other side of the hill, what has it got to do with us? That mountain must be three thousand feet high."

"Twenty-nine hundred thirty-three feet to be exact. Well, shall we investigate, or shall I leave you to cower behind Miss Bixley's skirt?"

"You know, Doc, if we wasn't about to risk our hides, I'd take a poke at you for that."

"I'll be happy to oblige you later, after we've had a look."

Raider unholstered his Colt and spun the cylinder. Taking a cartridge from his belt, he filled the empty chamber where the hammer had rested. He looked at Doc as he slipped the .45 back into his holster.

"Better check your Diamondback, Doc."

"I already have. Are you ready now?"

"Ready as I'll ever be."

The path was not steep as they ascended. Doc's torch illumined the narrow way. When the trail started to level out, Doc stopped and held the torch high overhead. They could see the entrance to the mine in front of them. The trees parted only slightly, where axes had felled the trunks of junipers and firs. The entire slope above the mine entrance was covered with rustling, shadowed foliage.

Raider peered toward the mine. "Think we ought to go in?"

"What do you think?"

"Hell, you're the captain of this expedition. If I was to have my way, I'd wait until morning."

Raider's hand reached for the charm that Red Claw had given him. It wasn't there around his neck. The damned Gypsy woman must've stolen it from him. Doc lowered the torch.

"I'm all for waiting," Doc said. "But not until morning. Let's sit still until we hear or see something."

"I'm waitin' with a full hand." Raider drew his Colt.

They watched the entrance to the mine for the better part of an hour. Doc's torch went out, leaving them in the darkness. As Doc was wrapping a piece of cloth around the end of the torch, the low, wailing voice came out of the mine.

"Turn back," it seemed to say. "All is lost. Turn back."

"That's good enough for me," Raider said. "I'm gettin' the hell out of here."

Doc grabbed his arm to stop him. "We've got to go in, Raider."

"I thought you might say that."

Doc struck a match and ignited the cloth on the end of the torch. He started slowly toward the entrance of the mine. He had drawn his .38 Diamondback, indicating that he was as scared as Raider, even if he didn't show it.

The opening into the mine shaft had been framed out with a crude archway of timbers. They paused at the aperture, listening. A rumbling sound echoed out of the shaft. Voices came behind the rumbling.

"It's darker'n hell in there, Doc. If we don't—"

"Turn back in the name of Satan!"

Raider jumped away from the mine's entrance. He looked up into the trees to see two arms of flame shooting out of the rocks, like Lucifer's own horns. Reflexively, Raider squeezed off a shot at the flames. The fire disappeared as quickly as it came.

"Raider, stop it, you'll scare off the—"

"Turn back, lost children," resounded the evil voice. "Turn back while you still have your lives."

Doc gripped the torch in one hand and the Diamondback in the other.

"Stand back," Raider said. "Afore you—"

A sulphurous, acidic smoke billowed out of the mine, poisoning the cool night air. Doc choked. He dropped the torch and held his hand over his mouth. Raider cried out and pointed up toward the mountain.

"You see that shit, Doc?"

Lights were spinning on the slopes above them. Like dancing feet of the Devil. Raider emptied his pistol at the ghostly apparition.

"You won't stop it like that," Doc cried.

"What the hell you want me to do?"

There was an explosive clap over the mine entrance. Jets of flame blasted up again. Smoke continued to flow out of the shaft. Raider pulled a bandanna out of his back pocket and tied it over his mouth.

Doc was gagging on the smoke. "Raider, we'd better turn back."

Raider picked up the torch and held it overhead again. Doc could see the maniacal gleam in Raider's black eyes. The big man from Arkansas wasn't scared anymore. He was angry.

"Raider, what are you—"

"I'm goin' in, Doc."

"I don't think it wise that we—"

Raider pushed past him, torch in hand, disappearing into the malevolent stench that issued from the mine's bowels. Doc started in after Raider, but the acrid vapor overwhelmed him. He staggered back out into the fresh air. His partner's cries echoed out of the mine, blending with the haunting voice that filled the murky night.

Raider charged through the smoke until he broke free of the foul mist. The sudden clearing of the air surprised him. He glanced back to see a smoldering pot that had been placed next to the opening of the mine. That sure as hell wasn't put there by any ghost. Raider turned around and looked back into the mine. He heard a multitude of sounds emanating from the cavernous recesses. As he moved toward the noise, he had to stoop down to keep from bumping his head on the ceiling of the mine shaft.

The mine broke into three directions. Raider paused at the intersection of three separate shafts. He listened, but he couldn't discern which corridor hid the bizzare noise of clinking hammers and muffled voices. The torch flickered and died, leaving Raider in the shadows. He expected to be overcome by pitch black, but instead an eerie red light illuminated the shaft.

"Doc!" he called. "Doc, stay back and cover me."

A dwarf turned the corner and looked up at Raider. His face resembled a snarling dog. Raider thumbed back the hammer of the Colt, but he couldn't pull the trigger. The dwarf spun around and ran back into the red light.

"Son of a bitch."

He followed the dwarf back into the shaft. The hammering sound had stopped. Raider slid around the corner into the red glow. He saw the monstrous figure clad in a red robe.

Raider remembered his days in Sunday school. "Jesus save me."

He was looking into the face of Satan himself. Long, curled

horns protruded from the wolfish head. Fur covered the snout and the long ears. White, canine teeth and slobbering lips.

Raider pointed the Colt at him. "Give it up," he heard himself saying.

Satan raised his hairy hands. Fire shot out of the sharp claws on the ends of the fingers. Raider staggered backward, his muscles frozen. He felt a pricking pain on his leg. The dwarf had stuck him with something.

Satan hissed and unleashed more fire from his fingers. Raider felt his head spinning. The Colt fell out of his hands. With his last ounce of strength he lunged forward, attacking the Devil in the red robes. His hand closed around the curled horn. Raider swung his fist, catching the canine snout with a hard right. The curled horn broke off in his hand. As he fell to the floor of the mine shaft, he heard Doc's voice echoing on the rock walls. Then he was no longer conscious, only lost in some vague, hideous nightmare.

When Doc pushed through the billowing smoke, he saw the red glow disappearing in a dark corner of the mine shaft. He followed the light to the first shaft that branched off the main tunnel, but when he gazed into the shaft, he saw that the red light had disappeared. Doc struck a match to illuminate the cavernous enclosure. The tunnel was a dead end, blocked by a wall of fallen rock. It was the same shaft that had collapsed on Hobert Bixley's partner, Lymon Partridge.

When the match burned his fingers, Doc dropped it and lit another. He stepped slowly through the tunnel, listening in the darkness. The sound of shallow breathing reached his ears. He felt his way along the tunnel wall until he found Raider lying on the floor, the Devil's horn still clutched in his hand. Doc tried to rouse him, but Raider was out cold.

"I suppose there's nothing to do but drag you out of here."

He grabbed Raider's shoulders and started to pull him along. He had to move slowly to find his way in the dark. As he neared the cave entrance, he heard the rumbling sounds within the mountain. Doc continued forward, past the smoking pot, through the timber archway into the fresh air of the night.

Doc let Raider's loose shoulders fall to the ground. Then

he gazed up at the mountain, waiting for something. A crescent moon was rising into the sky, casting an unearthly pallor on the treetops. Doc saw the shape as it soared toward the heavens. It was round and ominous against the starry sky. The orb sailed away into the night, disappearing behind the peak of the mountain.

Doc took off his derby and ran a hand over his sandy hair. "This will be a night to remember."

Raider was stirring on the ground. Doc hovered over him, wondering if he would live. When his black eyes opened, Raider cried out and lurched up.

Doc grabbed his shoulders. "Easy there."

"Satan, Doc. I saw Satan himself."

"I saw him too," Doc replied. "Although I daresay we can't be sure that we indeed saw Lucifer."

"Argue with this, Doc." Raider showed him the horn he had ripped from the wolfish head.

"I've no intention of disputing your claim, Raider. However, I suggest we go back to the house and discuss what we have seen. Can you walk?"

Raider tried to stand up with Doc's help. He managed to get to his feet, but his legs were wobbly. He staggered forward and then immediately threw up. He shook his head and leaned against a tree. His hand was holding his abdomen. "Boy, I'd really like to kill that little man, Doc."

"Which little man?"

"The one with the sledgehammer that's inside my stomach." Raider belched. "What did he hit me with?"

"I'd say an opium derivative, most probably. Your vomiting and nausea is also an indication that—"

Raider snorted. "Satan's magic! That's what hit me. You can't deny what I saw, Doc. You can't deny this."

Raider tossed the horn to Doc.

"I don't intend to deny anything. However, if you will follow me to the house, I think I can begin to explain some of this. Of course, you will have to tell me exactly what you saw. Providing you can remember the details."

Raider bent over and vomited again. He could recall the hideous sights all too well. Sights that he would rather forget.

• • •

"If it wasn't Satan himself, who was it then?" Raider asked.

They had been sitting at Diandra Bixley's dinner table, going over the facts. Miss Bixley and Tiny Delp were also with them, staring wide-eyed at Raider. Everyone but Raider had been drinking tea. He had thrown down several shots of whiskey that did nothing for the queasiness in his gut.

"Did you really attack the Devil himself?" asked Diandra Bixley.

"I guess you could say I did," Raider replied.

Tiny Delp laughed. "You're one brave cowpoke."

Raider shivered and poured himself a shot of red-eye. He ignored Diandra's attentive eyes. Fear, not courage, had egged him on. He wondered if he would repeat his actions, given a second chance.

"I don't deny that you saw something you believed to be Satan," Doc replied. "You could have been under the hallucinogenic influence of the drug they used to disable you."

"They?" asked Diandra.

"Old Pitch had a dwarf with him," Raider said. "And I didn't feel that pain in my leg till *after* I seen the Devil."

"And you say the dwarf had a dog's face?" Doc was taking notes.

"Yeah and Satan looked like a damn wolf with goat's horns." Raider shivered. "He's only got one horn now."

They all looked at the horn in the middle of the table. Doc picked it up and examined it again. Raider awaited his scholarly explanation.

"It's a goat's horn," Doc said. "Look closely. See the line of amber right at the base. Glue, animal glue. This could explain Satan and your dog-faced dwarf."

Diandra was puzzled. "That glue explains everything? How?"

Doc shrugged. "Masks. Easily constructed from the remains of dead animals. And that pot of smoldering smudge was by no means a supernatural device. It was simply tar that had been ignited."

"What about all of them weird smells?" Raider asked. "I smelt burnin' tar before and it didn't smell nothin' like that."

"Chemicals," Doc replied. "Mixed with the tar. Probably

some sort of sulphuric compound."

Raider was starting to listen. "Let's say you're right about the masks and the other stuff. How'd they get out of that tunnel without you seein' them? And how'd that ball rise up into the sky? Even if Satan did make himself a mask and a smudge pot, you tell me how he got out of that shaft and flew over the mountain to get away from us?"

Doc sipped his tea, pondering his reply to Raider's inquiry.

"As to the flying part," he said finally, "I would rather reserve my judgment on that until we have more facts. However, I must admit I'm stumped on how they were able to get out without coming out of the mine's front entrance. Mr. Delp, you worked the mine. Are there any exits other than the main opening? Say, perhaps, a tunnel that leads to another exit?"

Delp shook his head. "Nope. If there is, I ain't knowed about it."

"The map certainly shows nothing," Doc said. "What about the tunnel that collapsed on Lymon Partridge?"

"Must be a ton of rock piled up in there," Delp replied. "Don't see how nothin' human could've got out of there."

"That's cause nothin' human was in that tunnel," Raider said. "He shot fire off his fingers, Doc. And them voices— they wasn't human either. Not to mention that fire out of the rock and them lights up in the trees. How did that stuff happen?"

Doc raised a hand. "That is what we are here to find out."

Raider glared at his partner. "So what do we do next, Doc?"

"Well, I suggest a good night's sleep for everyone. Although I daresay none of us will sleep soundly tonight."

Doc rose and bowed to everyone. "I must go below to my wagon, to get some things that I require for this investigation," he said. "If you will excuse me."

Diandra touched his forearm. "Be careful, Mr. Weatherbee."

Tiny Delp got up. "Reckon I better go along with you. Ain't good for nobody to be walkin' around alone."

Doc went out with the small man dogging his steps.

Diandra turned to Raider. "Are you sure you're all right?"

He saw something in those caring eyes. She was admiring him. But then, women sometimes admired a man after he had struck up some danger. Raider poured himself another shot, deciding to ignore Diandra's mixed smoke signals.

"I'll live," he said. "Even if my stomach doesn't want me to."

"Would you like some sassafras tea? It's hot, and it might settle your nerves and your stomach."

"This'll do just fine." Raider threw back a shot of whiskey.

"Mr. Raider . . ."

"No need for the mister."

"Raider, I'm so glad that you and your partner have arrived. I feel . . . well, I just feel safer, and I know that you two can solve this mystery."

"Yeah."

He had wanted to say something like "Save the compliments for your friends," but he just didn't have it in him to be mean to her. Best just to keep his distance, he thought. He was in enough trouble already without trying to spark a proper woman. If you gave them a chance, fancy ladies could be just as much trouble as the Devil.

The inside of the mine didn't look as menacing in the morning light.

After a sleepless night, Doc, Raider, and Tiny Delp walked up the well-beaten path to the mine. Warm mists hung on the deep green lichens that grew between the evergreens. Fluttering birds raced through the morning air, gathering food and offering spring songs. It all looked hazy to Raider, who had tossed in a recurring nightmare of his devilish experience. Doc hoped to set him right by explaining the phenomena he had witnessed.

When they reached the mine's entrance, Doc reached into the shaft and pulled out the smudge pot. The tar had burned out, leaving a thin, enameled layer on the inside of the pot.

Tiny Delp was scratching his head. "How come we never found one of these pots, Mr. Weatherbee?"

"Beelzebub's exit was a hasty one last night," Doc replied. "Before he was always able to take this with him."

"I ain't never seen a pot like that," Raider said. "That's the Devil's hardware right there."

"Raider, this is a common utensil that can be purchased in any general store east or west of the Mississippi."

Delp nodded. "'Fraid your partner's right, cowboy."

"Watch your mouth, shorty."

"Raider!" Doc barked.

"Hell, I'm sorry, Delp. It ain't like me to run down somebody that's littler'n me."

"No offense taken," Delp said. "Listen, Mr. Weatherbee, I was wonderin' if you might let me stay out here until y'all have gone into the mine?"

Doc nodded. "I understand. Are there any lanterns about?"

"Right inside, on the wall. And listen, I'll stay right here by the entrance in case you need me."

Delp was happy to remain in the daylight. Doc and Raider took a deep breath before they slid through the timber-framed opening. Raider fumbled for a lamp on the wall. Doc flipped up a burning match and torched the end of the wick. He started to take out a cigar.

Raider bristled. "Forget it. I ain't breathin' that thing. Besides, it could interfere with other smells that might give us a clue."

"I defer, but only to the professionalism of your request."

"Does that mean you ain't gonna smoke that thing?"

"Correct," Doc replied.

Raider lifted the lamp and started back into the shaft. The first thing they saw was tracks on the sandy floor of the corridor. Raider looked closer to see hoofprints indented in the sand. Doc examined the tracks too.

"Cloven hooves," Raider said. "If that ain't the Devil . . ."

"Easy enough to fake," Doc offered. "A special shoe could be constructed. And look there, beside the hooves—the dwarf was wearing shoes. Leather soles from Hell? I doubt it, Raider."

"Okay, what about that red light? You call that natural?"

"I'll reserve my comments until after we've explored the mine completely."

"After you." Raider offered him the lantern.

"You picked a fine time to start being a gentleman."

Raider wore a wry smile. "Call it a fault, Doc."

Doc preceded Raider to the spot where he had grappled with the demon. Doc handed him the lamp and instructed him to hold it high. Raider watched as his partner scrambled around

on the floor of the mine, searching with a magnifying glass
that he had pulled from his pocket. Doc came right up the wall
with the glass. When Doc turned around, Raider saw that he
was smiling.

"What?"

Doc opened his hand. Raider looked down at the particles
of red. When he held the lamp closer, the particles glinted in
the light.

"Red glass," Doc said. "That's your red light. Simply put
a red glass cover on a lamp and you have a crimson glow from
the Inferno."

Doc pointed back at the wall. "And look there. See where
the chisel had been cutting. See the green flecks? Silver, Raider.
And if I'm right about the little I know of silver mining, there's
a larger deposit in this small wall."

"You sayin' Old Pitch was gettin' closer?"

"Well, I don't think he got everything he came for last
night."

"All right, then," Raider said. "I can see your point on some
of these things. But what about them balls of fire and them
lights on the mountain?"

"Give me time."

"And there's still that rumbling," Raider offered. "And the
way they got in and out of here like the wind."

"Let's have a look at the escape route."

The tracks led into the shaft where Hobert Bixley's partner
had met his death. Both sets of prints ended at a wall of rock.
Raider held the lantern next to the packed mound of stones.

"They'd never get through here," Raider said.

The flame flickered on the lantern.

"Look at that," Doc said. "The flame is disturbed by the
wind."

"Aw, that's just air from the entrance. This is the first tunnel
off the main shaft."

"Put the lamp low," Doc urged. "And stand in front of it,
to block any air currents."

Raider obliged him. The flame still flickered. Doc put his
hand up against the wall of stones. Air was flowing through
between the rocks.

"Raider, help me wedge out one of these stones."

"Doc, those rocks is stuck in there."

"Just humor me."

They tried, but none of the stones would come loose. Doc stood back and wiped sweat from his brow. How the hell had the silver thief gotten through the pile of rock?

"I'm finished in here, Raider. Unless you'd like to stay around and continue looking for clues."

"No thanks," Raider replied. "Just one other thing, Doc."

"What?"

"After Satan went through this rock, you saw him fly off again into the sky." Raider was wearing a half-smile.

"Yes."

"Ain't you ready to admit some of this might be magic?"

"Not at all," Doc replied, smiling. "Not at all."

"You think your partner's comin' up with somethin'?" asked Tiny Delp.

"Yeah, he always does," Raider replied. "Sometimes he's gotta be alone to cogitate on it. When he's ready, he'll talk our ears off."

They were sitting on Diandra Bixley's back porch, sipping whiskey. Doc had been upstairs by himself, locked in the loft with all his papers. Raider was glad that Doc did most of the brain work.

"Yeah, Doc's a right smart old boy," Raider said. "Course, I point up any holes in his schemes."

"This scheme's got a passel of holes in it."

"It does at that."

They drank until Diandra Bixley called them in to dinner. She had prepared a regal meal—fried chicken, biscuits, gravy, beans, bread, fresh tomatoes, and scallions. Raider was dipping a biscuit into a puddle of gravy when Doc ran into the room.

"Are you ready to listen?" Doc asked.

"You talk, I'll eat."

"Excuse me for interrupting your meal, Diandra, but I have to get this out and hear what Raider has to say."

"Of course, Mr. Weatherbee."

"All right," Doc said. "Now, without discounting Raider's

encounter with Lucifer, I will proceed in this direction: someone is stealing the silver from the mine."

Doc waited for Raider to say something, but for once Raider's mouth was full of food and unable to utter a single disruptive sound.

"Let's forget about the identity of our thief for a moment," Doc continued. "I'm going to go on my deductive powers and say that a *man*—a flesh and blood man, like any one of us—is stealing the silver from the Medicine Bow mine."

Raider swallowed and looked up. "Doc; how could a regular man—"

"Listen," Doc said. "Take another bite of those beans. I have more to tell you. You see, I believe that Satan, or the supernatural elements of the universe, are not responsible for the theft of the silver. Why would Lucifer, once God's brightest angel, need silver? The powers of evil work on the souls of men, not on a claim that's been in operation for ten years."

"Keep talkin'," Raider mumbled.

"Who would be able to pull off an operation such as this?" Doc asked. "Who would be able to convince the surrounding territory that the Devil himself is afoot? His performance even convinced Raider, who has seen more than his share of fakery and disguise."

"Hell, that's true." Raider looked up. "Oh, sorry for cussin', Miss Bixley. At the dinner table, I mean."

"Hush, Raider," Diandra said. "I want to hear the rest of this."

"Thank you," Doc rejoined. "Only a man of intelligence could devise a scheme of this sort. A man with a knowledge of science and artistry. A man—and this is most important—a man with the knowledge of this mining operation."

"An inside job?" Raider asked.

"Not someone presently with the company. With all deference to Mr. Delp and the men, I don't think they could pull off something this complex."

"Right about that," Delp said. "What about Short?"

"The disgruntled foreman?" Doc shrugged. "Well, it wouldn't surprise me if he was involved, but I hardly think he is the mastermind. No, the man who planned this scheme knew exactly what he was doing. He has been taking his time, waiting to strike, gathering his information to make sure that nothing can go wrong. I want you to see something."

Doc spread out a map on the table next to Raider.

"Be careful," Doc said. "Don't spill any gravy on it. Mr. Delp, I want you to see this too."

"What is it?" Raider asked.

"A map of the mine," Delp said.

"Exactly," Doc replied. "Now, look here. Do you see those red ink marks? Each one was marked by Hobert Bixley as a location for a heavy concentration of silver ore. All of these deposits were taken out. Am I right, Mr. Delp?"

"As far as I can see."

"Look at this black mark," Doc said. "Mr. Delp, can you tell me what that black mark represents?"

"Well, I ain't seen this map afore, but I'd say that was the next spot where we was supposed to dig."

"Precisely," Doc continued. "Had you started work there before these occurrences ran everybody out of the mine?"

Delp shook his head. "No."

"And according to the foreman's report, the deposit that you had been working was cleaned out by the thief. And Raider caught the perpetrator working on the next site. Only someone with knowledge of the mine would be able to go directly to the next spot on the map."

"Maybe Satan was readin' over the foreman's shoulder," Raider offered.

Doc thrust his hands into his pockets. "Are you going to take me seriously in this matter?"

"Hell, Doc, I seen Old Pitch shoot fire out of his fingers— I mean his claws." Raider wiped his mouth with the napkin that hung from his shirt.

"That's easy enough to explain."

"Yeah?" Raider scowled, biting into a chicken leg. "Let's see you do it."

"With Miss Bixley's permission."

She was enthralled. "By all means, Mr. Weatherbee."

Doc withdrew his hands from his pockets. Raider glanced up, chewing on his supper. Doc twirled his fingers and a ball of fire leaped into the air. Raider almost choked. Tiny Delp dived from the table. Miss Bixley was smiling at his parlor trick.

"How the hell did you shoot that fire off your hand?" Raider demanded.

Doc opened his fingers. "Flash powder and a match."

"That stuff stinks."

The stench of burnt powder lingered in the air. Raider was glaring at Doc. He wiped his mouth. "Dang me if you don't seem to have a handle on this thing, Doc."

"Then I've explained things to your satisfaction?"

Raider grunted. "Not everything. But you got my attention. Okay, if you think one man is doin' all of this, then I'm all for findin' him. Only trouble is, Doc, we ain't got a nibble on a suspect."

Doc turned to Miss Bixley. Diandra gasped and put a hand to her throat.

"Surely you don't think I'm the culprit, Mr. Weatherbee?"

"Of course not," Doc replied. "It's just that I will be needing your help. You see, I've put a few things together up in your loft."

CHAPTER NINE

Doc pulled up a chair and sat next to Diandra Bixley. Raider thought they looked pretty chummy, both of them smiling like foxes that had just gotten into a chicken coop. Raider slugged down a shot of whiskey from a bottle that had been brought to the dinner table by Tiny Delp. When Doc started to talk, Raider quickly forgot about Diandra's lovely eyes.

"As I said before, I don't believe that supernatural forces are at work in this case," Doc started. "All the phenomena can be explained, even though we haven't yet discovered all the sources."

Raider leaned over the table. "Is this leadin' to somethin', or are you just blowin' smoke?"

Doc ignored his sarcasm. "While I was upstairs going over the material given us by Diandra's father, I kept asking myself the same question. What kind of man would be capable of sustaining the illusion of a haunted mine? Raider, do you have any ideas?"

He really wanted Raider's opinion. The big man from Arkansas put a hand to his wrinkled forehead. His black eyes narrowed. "Hell, Doc, he'd have to be a smart hombre. Somebody like you that's read books and knows about things."

Doc raised his hand. "Exactly. A man with a knowledge of science. And a man who has seen the plans for the mining operation." He turned to Diandra. "I'm hoping that you can help me, Miss Bixley. Will you take a look at this list and tell me what you know about the names I have circled?"

The list bore the names of the past and present employees of the Medicine Bow Mining Company. Raider leaned forward and watched her eyes scanning the page. Maybe Doc had it figured. He usually did.

Diandra shook her head. "Billy Simpson was killed about six months ago, Mr. Weatherbee. They found him at the bottom of the mountain. Apparently he had taken a fall."

"And am I correct that he was a surveyor?" Doc asked.

"Yes. My father hired him to make charts of the mountain. He was hoping to find yet another vein of silver."

"What about the second name on the list?"

"Desmond Huther? He left us about the same time. He was a good man, and I can't tell you why he resigned."

Doc took her soft hand. "And he was simply a miner, nothing more?"

"Just as it says here," Diandra replied.

"Now the third name."

"Elton Wages was a geologist hired by my father. I think he came from a town nearby—Horton, I believe. He was a good man. He helped my father immensely."

"The record shows that he worked for your father for a month. He was paid handsomely—over five hundred dollars for his work." Doc handed the list to Raider.

Raider looked at it and threw it back. "Are you thinkin' he's our boy?"

Doc shrugged. "Horton is a two-hour ride south of here. Perhaps we should take a look for ourselves."

Raider scowled at Diandra. "How do you know all about these men? Seems like your daddy wouldn't exactly keep you posted on the dealin's of his mine."

"We are a close family," Diandra replied indignantly. "What my father doesn't tell me, my mother does."

"He was only asking," Doc rejoined. "What do you say,

Raider? We can be in Horton by tomorrow afternoon if we leave in the morning."

Raider stood up from the table. "Seems like the only thing we got. We could still be chasin' our own tails."

Diandra Bixley slammed her petite fist on the table. "Leave it to you to belittle Mr. Weatherbee's efforts!"

Raider grabbed the bottle from the table. "Doc, you better figure out what we're gonna do with this filly while we're gone."

"Raider, I think it would be best if—"

"If we left her for the ghosts and goblins," Raider replied. "I'm goin' for a stretch. Holler if you need me."

He stormed out of the dining room on his long legs. The others sat for a silent moment, listening to the clump of Raider's boots on the wooden steps outside. Diandra's face was bright red. Doc touched her hand but she pulled away.

"Honestly, I never thought I'd meet another man like him!"

"Another man?" Doc asked.

"You wouldn't understand."

She began to clear the table. Tiny Delp was shaking his head.

Doc turned to the little man. "Mr. Delp, I'll have to trust you with the security of the mine while we are gone."

Delp nodded. "I think me and the boys can handle it. Course, if that ghost shows up again . . ."

"Stay away from the mountain in any case."

"Mr. Weatherbee, I met this boy Wages. He didn't seem like no varmint to me, but he was a strange one. Thick glasses, no haircut, and he always seemed to be starin' off into nothin'."

Doc smiled. "Men of science are often eccentric. Did you by chance happen to work with him?"

"No sir. He spent most of his time with Mr. Bixley and Mr. Partridge. I guess he was tellin' them where to find more silver."

"He may have been doing a lot more than that."

They heard a crash in the kitchen. Diandra Bixley cried out.

Delp shook his head again. "I think your partner done got Miss Bixley's goat."

"That," Doc replied, "is the least of my worries."

• • •

Raider nursed the bottle as he headed down the trail through the woods. His ears detected the faint sound of chimes on the wind. The sun was low in the west, rendering orange and gray hues in the twilight. When laughter pervaded the forest, Raider spun and looked up toward the mountain. A hand fell on his shoulder. He brushed it back and filled his hand with the Colt.

"Go ahead and shoot me, cowboy," said the Gypsy woman.

The barrel of the .45 was trembling. "Damn you, witch-woman. How come you're always sneakin' up on me like a damned Injun?"

Her thick lips curled in a haughty smile. "I am like the mist, cowboy. I creep in when you least expect me."

"This business has got me spooked."

Her fingers slid over the barrel of the gun, roaming up Raider's arm to his chest. As he holstered the Colt, Medea's body pressed against his. She grabbed the bottle of whiskey and drank heartily. Raider smelled the rose oil in her musky black hair. Their mouths came together, mingling tongues and lips.

Medea's hand found the lump in his crotch. "I want it again, cowboy. I want your power between my legs. Will you give it to me? Can you forget about the Bixley woman?"

"She doesn't mean nothin' to me."

Medea laughed. "You are a bad liar, cowboy."

He pushed her away. "You think you know so much."

She pulled down her blouse, revealing her brown nipples. Raider drained the bottle and tossed it into the trees. He reached for the Gypsy woman, but she only laughed and ran away from him. Raider followed her along the path, to the clearing where her wagon rested. Shrill laughter mixed with the tinkling of the chimes in the trees.

"A north wind," she said. "The monster will not come tonight."

Raider grabbed her shoulders. "What do you know about the monster?"

"I know that you are a brave warrior, cowboy. You attacked the Devil himself. I know of your power."

Her hands went to work on the buttons of his fly. When his cock was in her hand, Medea pulled Raider's mouth to her breasts. His head was spinning from the whiskey and the taste of her dark skin. She fell back away from him and lay on the ground, pulling up her skirt to reveal the dark patch between her thighs.

"Hurry, cowboy. I want you inside me."

Raider lowered his body between her legs. She didn't even have to guide him in. Her cunt accepted the full length with the first plunging motion of his hips. She writhed beneath him, her fingers entwined in his thick black hair. A sweat broke over his body as he drove her ass into the bed of evergreen needles beneath them.

"All of it, cowboy. Give me all your power."

Raider's body shook as he climaxed in the soft folds of her womanhood. A hissing sound escaped from Medea's lips. Her hands gripped his buttocks, holding him inside her.

"My charm worked," she whispered. "I knew you would come to me."

He tried to roll off, but she wouldn't let him.

"You gonna keep me here all night?"

She licked her lips. "Yes. I will save you from the monster."

"Shiiit," he drawled. "You stole my Indian necklace. Is that how you wanted to save me?"

"Look at your neck, cowboy."

Raider reached into the folds of his shirt. Red Claw's charm was hanging in place around his neck. Medea laughed in his face.

"How the hell did you do that, woman?"

"I am your guardian angel. You cannot know."

He rolled off her, lying back on the ground. The wind stirred the chimes in the trees as darkness spread over the forest. Medea put her head on Raider's chest.

He grabbed her hand. "You ain't stealin' it from me again."

"I didn't steal it before," she replied. "You left here in a hurry. Do you remember?"

"Yeah, I guess so."

She raised herself on one elbow and looked into his eyes. "I fear for you, cowboy. I have gazed into my crystal ball, and I see you falling. I see a demon, a painted demon, hovering over you. I am afraid you—"

"Cut out that shit," Raider growled.

"Don't leave this mountain, cowboy. Don't go tomorrow."

"How did you . . . You were listenin' outside the window, weren't you?"

"Does it matter? Don't you believe me, cowboy? Don't you believe in the things I see?"

Raider touched the bear claw. "I ain't sure what I believe."

Her hand closed around the semi-erect shaft that protruded from his pants. "I'll keep you here. I'll keep you here all night. When I am through with you, you won't have the strength to go to Horton."

She kissed the line of hair down his stomach to his crotch. Her thick lips engulfed the head of his cock, causing him to spring back to life. As she worked on him, Raider thought she might just drain him of his energies. When the cool wind blew through the trees, he realized he didn't care what she did to him. Even if it took all night.

Raider felt warm sun on his sweaty head. He opened his eyes, expecting to see the Gypsy woman straddling his crotch, but she was nowhere in sight. As he raised up, he heard a twig snapping on the path. His hand reached for the holster that he had removed during the night. Thumbing back the hammer of the Colt, he turned the barrel toward the small figure on the trail.

"It's just me, Mr. Raider," said Tiny Delp.

Delp was staring at Raider's naked frame.

"What are you lookin' at, boy?"

Apparently Delp had never seen a man so well endowed. He turned away while Raider pulled on his pants. The Gypsy woman had not drained him. In fact, he felt better than he had before their night together. And Red Claw's charm still hung around his neck.

"How come you to walk down here, Delp?"

"Mr. Weatherbee sent me, sir. He saw somebody up at the mine this morning. He wants you to come before he—"

"Hell, let's get goin'."

Delp had trouble matching Raider's steps as they flew toward the house. Doc was waiting on the back porch, peering toward the mountainside with his extended glass.

Raider grabbed the telescope and scanned the trees himself. "Another demon?"

Doc shook his head. "I'm not sure. Is your Colt loaded?"

Raider handed him the glass. "Yeah. You ready?"

Diandra Bixley appeared behind them, holding her shotgun. Raider grimaced. "What you got on your mind, woman?"

"I'm going with you," she replied. "I feel I must do my duty in this matter."

"Hell no, you ain't!"

Doc gestured toward the path. "We have no time to argue, my friends. I suggest you stay behind us, Diandra. Shall we go?"

They hurried up the trail, stopping at the clearing where the trees parted. Doc peered toward the entrance to the mine. Raider had his hand on the butt of the .45. He forced Diandra back with a stern glance. He didn't trust a woman holding a scattergun.

When she was safely hidden behind a tree trunk, Raider turned around. "What the hell did you see anyway, Doc?"

"The figure of a man moving through the trees. He was . . . there! Did you see that?"

They both saw the flash of gray as it fluttered through the trees. Snapping and tromping in the brush, like something was coming out quick and it didn't care who heard or saw it. It seemed to be heading for the entrance of the mine. Raider thumbed back the Colt and let a round fly into the air.

"That's far enough, partner!"

The shot had startled Doc. "Raider, what the devil are you doing?"

"Let's find out what the hell is goin' on."

Raider started up the incline. The rustling continued on the slope above the mine shaft. Raider halted at the entrance to the mine, keeping his .45 trained on the forest above. A loud crash echoed through the trees, and suddenly it was tumbling down the steep angle. A bundle of gray fell out of the woods, landing at Raider's feet.

He pointed the gun at the smooth face of a startled young man. "Pinkerton National Detective Agency, mister. Don't you know you're trespassing?"

Doc came running up beside them. "I do believe he had the wind knocked out of him, Raider."

The man was gasping for breath. Doc slapped him on the back, helping him to fill his lungs. He had dark hair and a mustache like Raider's. His frame was tall, but without the width and sinew in the shoulders. Gray denim shirt and trousers, and shoes that Raider knew had been purchased back east. No hat.

"He's coughin' now, Doc."

Doc grabbed the young man under the armpits. "Let's get him on his legs and find out if he's friend or foe."

Raider kept the Colt raised as they lifted the young man to his feet. He leaned against one of the timbers that braced the mine's opening. His glassy brown eyes turned on Doc.

"I thank you, sir, for that slap on the back." He saw Raider's pistol. "I don't see any need for you to threaten me with that weapon, my friend."

Raider clenched his teeth. "We ain't friends yet. You ain't supposed to be stompin' around these parts without the permission of Mr. Hobert Bixley."

The young man started to reach into his pocket. Raider grabbed his hand. "Last man to pull a knife on me ain't pulled nothin' since."

"If you'd only let me—"

"You son of a bitch!" The woman's cry came from below.

A scattergun erupted, sending a load of buckshot into the wall above their heads. Loosened debris rained down on them. Raider turned back down the slope to see Diandra Bixley waving the smoke-spewing barrel. She aimed up at them and let the other barrel fly. The second shotgun burst sent her sprawling down the trail. More debris fell on Doc and Raider from overhead. Diandra jumped up and made motions of reloading the double-barrel.

"Have you lost your mind, woman?" Raider cried.

He flew down the path and grabbed the gun away from her. Diandra cried out again and scampered up the ridge. Doc watched her as she attacked the man in gray, pummeling him with her tiny fists. Doc finally managed to subdue her windmill flailing.

"Diandra, what's gotten into you?"

Raider stepped up with the .45 still pointed at the stranger. "Looks like these two have met before. Good thing she didn't kill you, partner. We mighta had to take her in for murder."

"I didn't mean to kill him," Diandra cried. "I was only trying to scare this rotten maggot."

"Hush your mouth," Raider said. "You're a lady. You ain't s'posed to talk like that."

"Just like a man to speak up for his own kind. Let go of me, Mr. Weatherbee."

"Only if you'll explain why you attacked this man," Doc replied.

She screamed and fought him for another minute before she gave out. Doc let go of her when she went limp. She was crying streaks of tears as she looked up at Raider.

"Remember, Raider?" Diandra said. "I told you before that I had once known a man like you. A man who asked me to marry him. A man who left me at the altar to seek his fortune elsewhere."

The man in gray was gaping at her. "Diandra, I didn't leave you at the altar. I faced you when I broke off our engagement. I simply wasn't ready for—"

"I hate you, Lye Partridge. I'll always hate you!"

Diandra ran down the path, back toward the house. Doc and Raider looked at the young man, who forced a smile. Raider put up the Colt again.

"Allow me to introduce myself, gentlemen. I am Lymon Partridge, Junior. My father was co-owner of this mine with Mr. Hobert Bixley. So I believe that when you accuse me of trespassing, you err. Instead, I should be accusing you of the same indiscretion."

He had been educated in the East, Doc thought. A clear speaking voice and a direct manner. Partridge reached into a pocket and produced a document giving him a half share in the Medicine Bow operation. Hobert Bixley had signed the title. Doc extended his hand.

"Perhaps we should retire to the house and discuss everything, Mr. Partridge."

"My friends call me Lye."

Raider grinned. "And some people who ain't your friends

no more. It's a good thing old Diandra there ain't a better shot."

Raider was the only one laughing as the three of them went back down the path to the house.

When Lye Partridge changed into a white shirt and tie, he looked rather sophisticated, Doc thought. He leaned back at the table, having devoured four eggs and a ham steak, and packed an English pipe with tobacco. Raider grimaced as Doc fished for an Old Virginia cheroot.

"Y'all are gonna smoke me out!"

Partridge lowered the pipe. "Dreadfully sorry, old boy."

Doc struck a sulphur match. "Pay him no mind, sir. He complains about everything if you let him."

But Partridge did not smoke, despite Doc's insistence. He replaced the pipe in his coat pocket and regarded Doc and Raider. Diandra Bixley was upstairs in her room. In her absence, Tiny Delp was playing cook.

Partridge leaned in toward Doc. "When I returned to Denver, Mr. Bixley informed me that my father had been killed. Are you here to investigate his death?"

Doc blew out a puff of smoke. "No. As far as we can see, your father's death was an accident."

"I see."

Raider glared at Partridge. "Didn't Bixley tell you about the spooks and haints up here?"

"He only said that there was trouble with the mine workers," Partridge replied. Then, after a pause: "Spooks and haints?"

Doc was regarding him out of the corner of his eye. "Yes, Mr. Partridge. It seems that someone is scaring the miners away in order to mine the silver at night. We did our best to apprehend the villain, but unfortunately we weren't quick enough."

Doc went on to inform Partridge of the details of Raider's encounter with "Satan." Partridge took it all in, showing little reaction. Raider kept an eye on him, waiting for a telltale sign of recognition.

"Extraordinary!" Partridge exclaimed at the end of Doc's tale.

Raider's eyes narrowed. "Sure as hell is, Partridge. And we figure a smart man is pullin' all of this. You seem pretty smart."

"Yes," Doc rejoined. "I'd say that you've traveled extensively, judging by the pipe and the inflection of your voice. And, I must add, your leaving Diandra seems to have caused a bit of harsh feeling between the two families."

Partridge laughed and shook his head. "I see what you're getting at. As far as my leaving Diandra, that is my own business. Let me say that I was young and headstrong, longing for.adventure in the world. When our fathers joined in a partnership, it was assumed that Diandra and I would be married. I was pressured into marrying her, but I couldn't go through with it. I respect her too much. I have returned here with the intention of making things right by her. That is, if she will have me."

Raider's feathers were ruffled. "That don't mean that you couldn't be slippin' in here to bilk your daddy's partner."

"Why would I steal what is already mine?"

Doc smiled. "Don't be insulted, sir. We are simply covering every possibility. And, of course, you can dismiss us any time you see fit."

Raider scowled at Doc. "What are you—"

"No," Partridge replied. "In fact, I want to aid you in the case."

"How you gonna help us?" Raider asked.

Partridge rose from the table. "If you will accompany me, gentlemen, I think I can help you explain at least two of the occurrences that have plagued this operation."

Raider looked at Doc for approval.

Doc shrugged and rose from the table. He stubbed out the cheroot and gestured toward the door. "After you, Mr. Partridge."

Lye Partridge preceded them out of the house. Raider stepped up next to Doc and spoke in a whisper. "Why'd you tell him he could throw us off the case, Doc?"

"If he truly were the perpetrator of this ugly business, he would have jumped at the chance to be rid of us."

"That's what I like about you, Doc. You're always thinkin'."

They followed Partridge up the path, back to the mine. Partridge halted in the clearing and pointed up the mountain. "I saw something up there, Mr. Weatherbee. I didn't understand it at first, but after you told me what has been going on around here, I think it might have something to do with those strange lights on the mountain. Of course, we'll have to climb."

Partridge went first, finding handholds that allowed him to climb up the steep angle into the trees. Doc removed his coat and came behind him.

Raider grumbled as he picked up the rear. "How the hell did you end up in these trees, Partridge?"

"I lost my way when I came up from the south."

Doc was puffing. "How did you get here?"

"I took the stage as far as I could and then walked."

They were silent the rest of the way, saving their energy for the climb. Each yard was a trek, grabbing the tree trunks, pulling up, and then scuffling a few feet to the next tree. Just when Raider thought he was played out, Partridge stopped in front of a rock formation. The trees had been cleared away with an ax. The opening could not be seen from below.

Partridge gestured toward the rocks. "I found this earlier, right before we crossed paths. It seemed strange to me, but I believe you'll find the source of your ghost lights in there."

Doc shuffled around in front of the rock formation. The stones had been stacked to create a cavern that was designed to house a complex apparatus. Doc reached in and pulled out the metal instrument. It consisted of three pinwheels and four candles. He reached in again to bring out a smoky mirror.

"What the hell is that?" Raider asked.

Doc's finger spun the pinwheels. "Incredible. See the melted wax? You simply light the candles and the hot air makes the pinwheels turn. As they spin, the light reflects off the mirror and throws dancing lights and shadows on the mountain."

"Son of a bitch," Raider said. "That's damned smart, all right."

Partridge was smiling. "If we go back down the hill, I think I can show you something else that might be pertinent."

"Lead on," Doc said.

Heading down the slope was easier. Doc left the pinwheels in place, in the event the criminals returned. He wanted above all to catch them in the act. It would be the easiest way to bring them to trial.

As they approached the slope above the mine shaft, Partridge stopped. "Take a look at this, Mr. Weatherbee."

Two metal pipes were extruding from the rock. Carbon smudge was built up around the ends of the pipes.

Doc touched the smudge with his finger. "Here are your shooting flames."

Raider tipped back his Stetson. "How'd they do that?"

"Probably by blowing powder through the end of the pipe," Doc replied. "Somewhere along this pipeline there's a candle or similar flame that ignites the powder on the way out. And it also confirms something I've suspected all along—another open tunnel somewhere in this mine."

Raider looked at his partner. "And probably a third man to work all of these contraptions while the other two dig out the silver."

Doc nodded. "I wouldn't be surprised. If we searched long enough, we'd no doubt find a secret entrance to that tunnel from this side of the mountain."

Partridge was frowning. "The tunnel where my father was killed."

"Yes," Doc replied. "It may have been sabotaged in order to provide the thief an entrance and exit that no one would suspect."

Raider's brow wrinkled. "Hell, Doc, we couldn't find a way through that wall of rock. And if what you're sayin' is true, there must be a tunnel that comes out somewhere on the other side of the mountain. How else would somebody be able to get in and out?"

"I soon may be able to answer all your questions, Raider. Mr. Partridge, I would appreciate it if you would continue to look for the hidden entrance to the mine."

Partridge nodded. "I'll be happy to assist you in any way I can."

"We have an appointment in Horton, Raider. We've lost precious time already. And I want to take my wagon along. I may need all my tricks to do battle with this wizard."

Raider felt a shiver running the length of his spine. He wasn't really sure what a wizard was, but he sure as hell didn't like the sound of it. He started to ask Doc to explain but then decided he would just as soon not know.

CHAPTER TEN

Doc and Raider rode hard to the south, breaking out of the woodlands into a bumpy plain that stretched toward Horton, Colorado. They reached the brown, disintegrating hamlet by late afternoon. Raider thought Horton could have been any one of a hundred towns that hadn't prospered west of the Mississippi River. Speculators had bought up the land, hoping the railroad would turn through the area and bring in boom-town money. But according to the sheriff, the big money had never come to Horton. And as far as he knew, neither had a man named Elton Wages.

"Ain't seen nothin' of a ..." The aging lawman ran a hand over his thin scalp. "What'd you call this Wages fellow?"

"A geologist," Doc replied. "A scientist who studies rocks and landscape formations. He would have been working in the silver mines north of here."

The sheriff's gray eyes showed recognition. "That'd be the Medicine Bow Company. I heared of them, even if they ain't brought a single dollar into this town. Course, as long as they keep payin' my wages, I'll stay on here as sheriff."

Raider stared at the old man. "Who's 'they,' sheriff?"

140

"Town council. Ain't many of 'em left, though. Don't know where they keep gettin' the money."

Doc cleared his throat and gazed blankly out of the smoky window in the sheriff's office. "Sheriff, how are you dealing with the reports of strange objects in the sky?"

The old man tipped back his hat and narrowed his gray eyes. "Stranger, I ain't crazy enough to take that bait."

Doc turned back toward the sheriff. "Bait? Sir, as I told you before, we are operatives of the Pinkerton National Detective Agency. We aren't trying to trick you, we simply want to know the truth. Now, have you had reports of strange objects in the sky?"

The sheriff finally nodded reluctantly. "Yes, sir. But I can't say that I've seen this thing myself."

Raider looked baffled. "Hell, ever'body's goin' loco around here."

"Not necessarily," Doc replied. "Sheriff, have you any knowledge of land purchases in this area, say in the past year?"

"Just the old Barlow place. I heard the railroad people bought it, but no railroad ever come this way. It circled on up to Cheyenne and then went on west from there."

"And you never heard of a man named Wages?"

The sheriff's brow wrinkled. "What'd you say he looked like?"

"Eccentric, longish hair, thick spectacles, absentminded."

"Can't say that I have, Mr. Weatherbee."

Raider leaned in toward the sheriff. "The Medicine Bow Company has a paper that lists Wages's home as this town. Now, you sayin' you don't know him might mean, hell, what do you call that, Doc?"

"Complicity," Doc replied.

"Yeah, complicity. And that means if you're mixed up in this business that you stand a good chance to hang alongside them that's guilty."

The sheriff smiled and shook his head. "Partner, I hear you, but it ain't reachin' me. I ain't done nothin' but sheriff this one-wagon town."

Doc took over. "Then we can count on your cooperation to the letter of the law?"

"Yes, sir. I got respect for you Pinkertons."

"Good," Doc replied. "Do you know where the old Barlow place is located?"

"Yes, I do."

"Then I want you to ride there for us. Tell whomever you meet that two Pinkertons were here asking you questions about several strange incidents. Ask the residents of the Barlow place if they have seen or heard anything out of the ordinary. No matter what they say, tell them that the Pinkertons have given up on finding anything and that we sent a wire to our home office saying that we are removing ourselves from the case. Furthermore, tell them that you are pretty sure that the Medicine Bow mining operation has been closed down permanently. Have you got all of that?"

The sheriff was frowning, trying to remember everything. "Maybe if you ran me through it one more time."

Doc made him repeat it until it came easily. Raider just watched, wondering if the old man would be able to pull it off. When the sheriff finished his final recitation, Raider tapped Doc on the shoulder.

"What the hell are you aimin' at?"

"If I am wrong, nothing," Doc replied. "If I am right, then perhaps we can catch our culprit in the act. Sheriff, is there someplace that we can observe the Barlow place without being seen?"

"There's a ridge above there, ain't got no name, but it looks right down on the barn and ever'thin'."

Doc clapped his hands together. "Very well, we shall move at once. I do hope we have a south wind tonight."

"Why's that?" asked the sheriff.

Raider grunted. "A south wind brings up the demons, Sheriff. Didn't you know that?"

The look in the old man's eyes told Raider that he knew all too well.

In the keen glow before twilight, Doc and Raider watched the sheriff as he invaded the Barlow place. Doc held his telescope to his eye, gazing down on the three buildings that sat in the middle of the basin land. The largest structure—some kind of barn—attracted most of his attention. It was there that the sheriff spoke to the tall man. Doc wished he could see the

THE GHOST MINE 143

man's features, but at such a distance even the telescope was useless.

Raider tapped at the ground impatiently. "What's he doin'?"

"Talking, as far as I can see. There, he's getting on his horse. Apparently he's finished."

Raider took the telescope from Doc. "He's comin' back this way just like we told him. I guess that means he ain't in cahoots with 'em. If that's *them* down there."

"Keep watching the barn, while I talk to the sheriff."

In ten minutes the sheriff had joined them on the ridge. He was puffing excitedly. Probably not used to such intrigue, Doc thought. Doc offered him a slug off a whiskey flask.

The sheriff drank and handed the flask back to Doc. "I done like you told me, Mr. Weatherbee."

"Did you see the man I described to you?"

"Yes, he answered the door on that barn when I knocked. Only he didn't do no talkin'. It was another man, a tall fellow."

Doc nodded. "I saw. What did you learn about him?"

"Nothin' much. He was older but still spry. He just listened to what I said. Told me he hadn't seen nothin' strange. When I asked him what he was doin' in these parts, he just thanked me and closed the door."

"And you made sure you told him that Raider and I were off the case?"

"I did."

"Very good, I hope that—"

Raider called from the ridge. "Doc, you better come up here and take a look at this."

Doc hurried up to the crest of the ridge with the sheriff in his tracks. Raider offered him the telescope. Doc peered down at the barn. He watched as the doors opened and three men dragged out a huge, square object. One of the men stood at least two feet shorter than the others. A dwarf. Doc handed the glass back to Raider.

"Tell me what you see."

Raider described what he witnessed through the telescope. "Hell, looks like a damn basket to me. And, hey, there's a midget with them other two boys. Now they're goin' back into the barn and bringin' out somethin'." He waited a moment, still peering at the scene. "Hell, it looks like some kinda . . .

cloth, I reckon. And the little one is draggin' the end of it."

"There's your eye of Satan," Doc said.

Raider took the glass away from his eye and looked back at his partner. "What are you talkin' about, Doc?"

Doc took the telescope and looked through it again. "A balloon, Raider. That's how our culprit has been traversing the distance between here and the mine. Probably hot air, as the transportation of hydrogen would be difficult in such a remote area."

Raider took off his Stetson. "A balloon, huh? Seems like an awful lot of trouble just to steal some silver."

"No trouble at all for a genius. One of those men down there has a keen mind. That is why I suggest caution in dealing with him."

The sheriff asked for the glass. "Pardon my ignorance, Mr. Weatherbee, but I ain't sure I know what you're talkin' about."

Doc put his thumbs in his vest pocket. "A balloon, sheriff. A lighter-than-air craft. Invented by two Frenchmen, the Mont-golfier brothers. Usually constructed of light cloth, linen, or silk. The first manned flight was made by a man named Rozier and a marquis whose name I cannot recall. You see, hot air or certain gases will cause the balloon to rise. A basket underneath is attached by ropes allowing passengers and cargo. They were used for surveillance in the War Between the States."

Raider was skeptical. "How can they go back and forth so easy?"

"The wind," Doc replied. "All of the 'satanic' visits to the mine occurred when the wind was blowing from the south. The visits ended when the winds shifted and blew in the opposite direction."

The sheriff was shaking his head. "Ain't it a wonderment."

Raider's stomach kicked up a gurgling noise. "Son of a bitch."

"What's wrong with you?" Doc asked.

"Nothin'."

Raider was remembering something the Gypsy woman had said. Something about flying and then falling. Maybe she was in on the whole thing. Maybe . . . maybe he had better stop thinking about it.

"There it goes," Doc said. "What a fantastic sight. I'd give

THE GHOST MINE 145

anything to study that mechanism. I've never seen a balloon raised so fast."

Below them the team of three worked to hoist the fabric on a pulley. When the balloon was hovering over the basket, the dwarf stuck a torch into a metallic container in the basket. Quickly the dark orb began to fill up with warm air.

Doc shook his head in admiration. "A pity that such a mind has been turned to crime."

Raider was scratching his head. "Doc, somethin' I don't understand. How do they get that thing up and down? I mean, if they was totin' silver, wouldn't that weigh them down?"

"Ballast," Doc replied. "They use bags of sand to weigh down the balloon and then discard them in lieu of the silver on the trip back. I'm also guessing that he can adjust the flow of hot air."

Raider looked up toward the red sky. "Gonna be dark soon."

"We'd better be going," Doc said.

"Back to the minin' camp?"

Doc shook his head. "No, I want to ride north and stay on this side of the mountain. Sheriff, I would appreciate it if you would take this envelope and relay the message to our home office if we aren't back in your office by tomorrow morning."

"That's all you want from me, Mr. Weatherbee? Then I'll be happy to oblige. Anythin' to keep from tanglin' with that . . . thing down there."

Raider knew how he felt. "You're plannin' on followin' that thing, ain't you, Doc?"

"Not exactly," Doc replied. "I want to precede it. If we wait in the right spot, we'll be able to find the back entrance to the mine. Sheriff, may I borrow your mount? I'll leave my wagon as collateral."

The sheriff nodded. "Wind's blowin' up from the south."

Raider turned up his collar. "Sure as hell is."

Doc tipped back his derby. "Do you know what that means, gentlemen?"

They both shook their heads.

"Tonight," said Doc, "the monster dies."

Raider clutched the Indian charm around his neck, trying to forget the words of the Gypsy woman.

• • •

They rode to the base of the mountain, arriving just after dark. Raider leaned back in a rocky hollow, keeping his eyes trained on the sky. At least there would be a moon, he thought. The silvery crescent was rising slowly on the horizon. Doc had his telescope extended.

"Think he's gonna come tonight?" Raider asked.

"If he took the bait. And judging by their preparations, they have the hook firmly in place."

Raider shook his head, still clutching the red claw around his neck. "Hell, Doc, we got us a corker here. Dead bodies all over the place. The foreman and Lye Partridge's father. You think that Wages feller is the one?"

Doc sighed and put down the glass. "We only have a description of the geologist and the sheriff's verification of that description. Something else is worrying me."

"Don't hold nothin' back."

Doc raised the glass again. "There was a third man helping with the balloon. We have no clue as to his identity."

"What about the other two men on that list you had?"

He shook his head. "One of them is dead, the other took off. No, I submit this hypothesis for your consideration. Someone approached all three men on the list with this plan to steal the silver. One of them, Wages, accepted the offer. The other two turned him down. One of them was killed, and the other fled before he could be killed. Hence the disappearance of two men on the list, the third being Wages, who is still in league with the mastermind of the operation."

Raider blew on his hands, which were icy from the night air. "How about young Lye Partridge? You think he's got somethin' to do with all this?"

"Doubtful. Perhaps Short, the man you ran off, was helping. He certainly seemed like a disruptive factor."

Raider nodded. "Yeah, that makes sense. Could Short have been that third man with the balloon?"

"I would have recognized him. No, we will have to apprehend our third man before we can identify him. I must admit I'm at a loss to even guess who he might be."

The wind came up on them from the south, increasing in velocity. Doc handed the glass to Raider, ordering him to keep watch while Doc made a fire. The flames warded off the unwelcome coolness of the mountain night. Doc looked up at the steep slope that rose above them. If the balloon was going to land anywhere, it would have to be on a ledge above them.

Raider lowered the glass and hunkered by the fire. "It's still damned spooky. You never know who might be runnin' around in these mountains. Old Red Claw might be lurkin' nearby."

Doc raised the telescope. "Is that why you've kept your hand on that pendant? Hoping for some luck, are you?"

"I might be. I've always said it's better to be lucky than good. If I have a choice, I'll take the lucky break every time."

Doc suddenly kicked dirt on the fire.

"Hey," Raider said, "I was just gettin' warm."

"I hope your pendant is working, Raider. I think our luck just ran out. We're on our own from here."

Doc pointed toward the sky. Raider looked up to see the ghostly reflection against the moon glow. A silhouetted orb hung low over the peaks of the mountain. Doc's plan had worked. Raider only hoped he had a plan for dealing with the demon in the heavens.

"What do we do now, Doc?"

"Let them land first. When we see where they are, we can make our move."

Raider drew his Peacemaker and leaned back against the rock. He had attacked Satan once to no avil. This time, however, he planned to do a lot more than grab Old Pitch's horn.

CHAPTER ELEVEN

Doc and Raider leaned against the wall of rock, hiding in the moon shadows as the balloon settled in above them. Doc couldn't see how many men were directing the craft, but he thought he detected three distinct voices in the faint echo. A hissing sound also filled the air, like steam escaping somewhere. The noises went on for the better part of an hour, and then a rumbling vibrated through the mountain.

"Raider, I believe we can move freely now."

Raider leaned back away from the slope. "You think they left somebody to stand guard?"

Doc also stepped back and gazed up the mountainside. He could see the shadowy orb, fixed by lines over a protruding ledge. Wages, the geologist, had probably found a natural tunnel that could be linked to the first shaft that had been cut by Bixley and Partridge.

"They didn't get up there by balloon the first time," Doc said.

Raider frowned at his partner. "What are you jawin' about?"

Doc started to feel his way along the base of the slope.

"When our intelligent adversary discovered this cavern, he was no doubt on foot. There must have been a way for him to get up there by climbing."

"And we're supposed to find it in the dark?"

"Stop grumbling and whip up a torch."

Raider found dried twigs and wrapped his bandanna around the bundle. Doc ignited the end with a sulphur match. When the torch was burning, Doc glanced back up at the balloon's swinging basket.

"Any movement up there?"

Raider's eyes were straining in the half-light. "I don't see nothin'."

They started looking again for a way to ascend the slope. Doc made his own torch, and they branched out in two directions. The search was beginning to look hopeless when Doc heard Raider's night-owl screeching. For a second the signal cry bristled the hair on the back of Doc's neck. He marked the direction in the dark and headed for the dim glow of Raider's torch.

Raider was studying something in the rock. "I think I got it here, Doc. Looks like somebody carved some handholds. Wages maybe?"

Doc saw the indentations leading up the steep wall. "Hard to say. These could have been carved here by Indians a hundred years ago. Do you think you can make the climb?"

"Me?"

"I'll stand guard down here to make sure no one attacks you from the rear."

Raider emptied his lungs. "Son of a bitch if I don't get all the chicken-pluckin' work."

"If you're afraid, we can look for another way up."

Doc knew the challenge would be answered. Raider fitted his fingers into the first handhold in the rock. After another deep breath, he was on his way. Doc listened as he grunted up the wall, taking the slope a foot at a time. The balloon looked to be about five hundred feet up on the mountain. Raider disappeared in the shadows, leaving Doc alone in the moonlight. Doc's pocket watch recorded the passage of an hour before the night-owl call filled the air.

Doc backed off to see Raider standing in a dim glow that emanated from the balloon. Something shot out from the glow and slapped the side of the mountain. A rope. Raider had performed with his usual professional expertise. Doc grabbed the tether and scaled the sheer cliff.

"You gotta see this," Raider said as he pulled his partner onto the ledge.

Doc eyes fell on the apparatus of the sky craft. A blue flame burned in a baffle that pointed up into the heart of the balloon. Protruding from the corners of the basket were four metallic vents that seemed to be connected to the firebox in the center. Doc fought the urge to hop into the basket for a closer examination of the mechanism.

"Extraordinary! He's using some sort of natural fuel to heat the air that makes the balloon rise. And there's a container for water somewhere near the heat, producing steam. Do you see, Raider? He can influence the swing and direction of the balloon by releasing steam jets."

Raider was staring at the entrance to the tunnel. "If you say so, Doc. Maybe we oughta have a look-see in the shaft."

Doc nodded, tearing himself away from the magnificent work of science. He followed Raider to the opening that led down into the Medicine Bow silver mine. A set of steel tracks lay on the floor of the tunnel. The rumbling sound had come from a mining cart on the tracks.

Raider thumbed back the hammer of his Colt. "You sure as hell had this pegged, Doc. Want me to go first?"

Doc's hand was full of his .38 Diamondback. He shook his head and started ahead of Raider into the dark, rocky corridor. The tunnel had to be either natural or the work of Indian tribes. In the period that it had taken to set up the haunting ruse, no one could have fashioned such a long shaft into the mountain.

They descended in the blackness, following the length of the tracks. Doc kept his hands on the walls until he felt a change in texture. When he struck a sulphur match, he saw the pick marks in the rock. The tunnel narrowed until it was barely big enough to allow passage of a small cart.

"This is where they made the connection," Doc said.

"Looks like we're gonna have to crawl."

They went belly down for fifteen or twenty feet until the tunnel opened up again and allowed enough room to walk upright.

Raider saw the light ahead of them. "We made it, Doc."

Doc didn't need a match to appreciate the extent of the work. The collapsed tunnel had been cleared, with only a wall of carefully laid rocks to sustain the illusion of an impasse. A section of the rock was designed to open up when the mining cart triggered the mechanism. Only the weight of the cart could open the crawl space into the mine. Doc went first through the aperture. Raider squeezed behind him into the adjoining tunnel.

A red glow filled the mine shaft. Doc raised his .38 Diamondback and held a finger to his lips. Raider nodded and followed along quietly into the main tunnel. Clinking sounds of steel on stone reached their ears. They rounded the corner to find Satan at work. The broken horn had been replaced on his hairy head.

"Good day, sir," Doc said. "I am Doc Weatherbee of the Pinkerton National Detective Agency. I am afraid that I must take you into custody for the unlawful mining of this silver."

The Satan figure roared with a lion's howl. From the folds of a red robe he produced a ball of fire that flashed toward Doc and Raider. The dwarf was hiding behind his master, peering out as Doc's laughter echoed through the tunnel. Raider didn't find anything humorous.

"A nice trick," Doc said to the wolfish face. "However, you are not the only one with resources."

Doc waved his hands and returned the ball of flame, singeing the Devil's costume. The demon slapped at the smoldering tips of hair, staggering backward. Raider took aim with the Colt.

Doc pushed Raider's hand away. "No. We don't have to shoot him. Sir, if you'll take off that ridiculous costume . . . Mr. Wages, is it?"

The demonic figure hesitated for a moment. Raider lifted the Peacemaker again. Satan reached for his horns and withdrew the bizarre head/mask from his shoulders. Doc had anticipated the bespectacled geologist described to him by Tiny Delp. Instead, he looked upon a handsome, gray-haired man.

"My hat is off to the Pinkertons," the man said.

Raider was gaping. "Who the hell are you?"

"I've seen this man before," Doc said. "Or someone who looks like . . . of course, the family resemblance is incredible."

"Doc, you want to let me in on this?" Raider asked.

Even in the red light, Doc could see it. "Raider, allow me to introduce Mr. Lymon Partridge. No longer deceased."

The man laughed. "How smart you are, Pinkerton. I should never have underestimated you."

Raider's eyes narrowed. "Why, Partridge? Weren't you happy enough to have a share of the silver? How come you thought you had to have it all?"

Partridge laughed insanely. "Half, did you say? This claim is mine. I found it. Hobert Bixley was simply tagging along. He managed to file the claim first, before I could get to the assay office."

"But he filed it under both names," Doc replied. "And according to Mr. Bixley, you shared expenses in your prospecting."

"He lied, Pinkerton! All of them lied to me. Do you understand?"

Raider leaned in toward his partner to whisper, "He ain't all here, Doc. Let's get him out of here."

Doc nodded. "Let me see if I can talk him out. Mr. Partridge?"

"How the hell did you recognize me, Pinkerton?"

"Your son," Doc replied "He's here. You'll find him below at the main house. If you'll come along . . ."

Partridge shook his head. "Son? The ungrateful son who left for parts unknown? I have no son, Pinkerton. I am alone. Alone with my silver." He held up a chunk of rock. "Look at it. White as snow. Pure."

"Remarkable," Doc said. "I daresay that you had little trouble convincing Elton Wages to mastermind this scheme."

Partridge's smile was eerie. "Wages is a genius. I merely suggested this to him. He planned everything. The cave-in, my faked death."

"And you found the connecting tunnel by accident?" Doc asked.

"Yes. You're very good, Weatherbee. Perhaps we should

all throw in together. I'm offering you—"

"The way you offered Simpson and Huther? You killed one of them and drove off the other. And then you recruited Short. How much did he help you?"

Partridge laughed. "How did you figure all of it out?"

"He's a goddamn genius," Raider replied. "Now you better move along, Mr. Partridge. We got to take you in. Then we got to go get your man Wages. Don't worry, you'll get a fair trial."

Partridge shook his head and laughed.

"This is no laughing matter, sir," Doc said. "I suggest you come along. You've played your last trump card."

"Have I, Mr. Weatherbee?"

A rifle lever chortled behind them. "Drop them irons, Pinkerton scum."

The dwarf stepped out brandishing a sawed-off scattergun. Raider looked back over his shoulder to see Short standing behind them with a Winchester aimed at his head. They were covered front and back.

Doc dropped his Diamondback. "You'd better do as they say, Raider."

"Fuck these varmints."

"Just do it."

Raider's Colt hit the floor of the mine shaft. Partridge gestured toward the firearms. The dwarf moved forward to pick up the pistols.

"Why, look at that little ole pissant," Raider said.

The dwarf glared up at him. Doc could not believe what happened next. Raider grabbed the little man and picked him up, lifting him over his head. He spun and threw the dwarf toward Short's Winchester. When the little man struck him, Short fell backward. Raider dived for his Colt. Doc leapt backward, picking up the sawed-off scattergun. He moved around behind Short.

"How about that?" Raider said. "We done outfoxed the Devil again."

"Raider, look out!"

Short came up with the Winchester. Doc kicked at the barrel, throwing the shot off target. The rifle erupted, sending a lead

slug into the ceiling of rock overhead. A trembling shook the
mine shaft as a load of dirt and stone collapsed on top of Short.
Raider clung to the side of the wall until he felt a sharp pain
in the back of his neck. Partridge had struck him from behind.
Raider fell to the floor of the shaft, his head spinning. He was
conscious, but he couldn't move.

Partridge shouted at the dwarf. "Brutus, hurry up to the
balloon."

"I'm going to kill the Pinkerton," replied the high voice.

Raider felt the barrel of a gun against his temple.

"No!" Partridge cried. "Another shot might bring down the
rest of this tunnel. Just do as I say."

Raider listened as the little man scampered out of the tunnel.
Partridge hovered over him, working something in his fingers.
Raider heard a fizzling sound, and then he saw the red stick
of dynamite fall beside his face.

"Goodbye, Pinkerton. Perhaps you will meet the real Satan
on the other side of darkness."

His footsteps diminished as he left the tunnel. Raider struggled to regain his senses. He smelled the sulphur of the burning
fuse. His hand came up to grip the red shaft. The fuse was
long, but it was burning down fast. Raider felt a hot pain in
his palm as he ripped the fuse out of the dynamite stick.

"Son of a bitch."

He managed to sit up. His whole left side was numb. He
peered through the dust at the wall of rock that separated him
from Doc. There wasn't much choice. If he could get to his
feet, he had to follow Partridge. What a crazy bastard, he
thought, stealing what was already his. Some of the numbness
was leaving his extremities as he struggled to stand up.

It was slow going through the tunnel. He crawled upward,
traversing the corridor that had been used to connect the two
shafts. Hours seemed to pass, each step a major effort. He
finally heard the voices and the hissing steam. As he stumbled
toward the cave entrance, he heard Partridge telling the dwarf
to hurry.

He had to stop them. He had to try, at least. Raider came
up out of the tunnel, into the fresh air of the moonlit night.
The balloon was rising off the ledge. Raider staggered toward

a line that dangled from the basket. He grabbed the rope and looked around for one of the metal cleats that had been fixed in the rock. Quickly he fashioned a knotted loop, reaching for the cleat that was a few feet away. The balloon soared abruptly, lifting him off the ledge. He clung to the line as the sky craft rose into the heavens.

Raider wondered if they felt his extra weight. A couple of sandbags flew over the side. His arms were aching. He climbed up the rope and hooked his boot heel in the loop he had made.

The view was incredible. Below them loomed the peaks of the forested mountain. Raider thought he saw the moon's reflection on a slick surface. A mountain lake, perhaps. He looked back up toward the basket. He would hang on, damn it! He would hang on until they landed, and then he would shoot everybody.

"Look!" came the cry from above.

The balloon swung in an eddy of wind. Raider felt a vibration on the rope. Brutus, the dwarf, was hanging over the side of the basket, sawing at Raider's lifeline. Raider reached for his holster but found it empty.

"You bastard! You little bastard!"

He looked down at the silvery reflection below him. It had to be a fifty-foot drop. Above, the dwarf continued with the knife. Raider prayed that it was a lake below him. The line broke and he plummeted into the darkness. His feet struck the surface of the water, breaking his fall.

He sunk downward, cold black water engulfing him. His sense remained, but he felt suddenly immobile. A pain shot through his ankles. Something had a hold on his feet. He looked up at the surface of the water, which was only a yard from his face. He struggled, holding his breath, trying to dislodge his feet from the mucky bottom of the mountain lake.

His lungs ached. Water had filled his boots, creating a suction that kept his feet imprisoned. Air bubbled up from his mouth, disturbing the water's surface. He cried out in one last futile breath. But no one could hear him, not below in the cold lake. His last ironic thought before he lost consciousness was that he could see the sliver of a crescent moon, rising high in the star-spattered firmament.

* * *

When the tunnel collapsed on Short, Doc fell back away from the debris. As the dust settled, he saw that he had been separated from his partner. He listened but could not hear anything. He wondered if Raider was alive.

Doc bolted out of the mine entrance, running down the path to the main house. He found Lye Partridge and Diandra Bixley tied up in wooden chairs. Tiny Delp and his crew lay nearby, shot in the back of the head by Short. Doc removed the gag from Lye's mouth.

"He came up on us without warning, Doc."

Doc nodded. "I know. He caught us from behind. Did you hear the shooting down here?"

"No. Where's your partner?"

Doc hesitated. "I don't know."

He untied Lye, who then released Diandra. She rubbed the rope burns on her wrists. "I should have killed Short when I had the chance," she said.

"He's gone," Doc replied. "A ton of rock fell on him."

Diandra put a hand to her throat. "Raider? Did he..."

"I said I don't know!" Doc snapped. Then: "I'm sorry, both of you. It's just that...I think they may have done him in."

Lye put his hand on Doc's shoulder. "Who are they, Mr. Weatherbee?"

"The men who have been stealing the silver," Doc replied. "Lye, I think you'd better sit down."

Lye's brow was fretted. "Tell me now, Weatherbee. Tell me."

"Your father isn't dead."

"What?"

"But I'm afraid he isn't exactly...right. Something has snapped inside him. If you'll just sit quietly and listen..."

Doc explained the way Lymon Partridge had enlisted the aid of Elton Wages, the way they had set up the supernatural occurrences. When he was finished, Lye leaned forward and put his face in his hands. Diandra touched his hair, patting his head.

"Lye, if you'll—"

"The silver," Lye said. "That's what drove him to it. He

was a poor man all his life. It wasn't he who found the claim, Mr. Weatherbee. It was Diandra's father. He was kind enough to share with my father. I guess he resented Mr. Bixley's graciousness. I don't know. He wasn't right after the war. He was never a strong man."

Diandra took his hand. "I'm sorry, Lye. I'm truly sorry."

Lye looked up at Doc, who was staring out the window. "What next, Mr. Weatherbee?"

"Horses," Doc replied. "I must find a fresh horse and go after your father. I can send a wire to the home office in Horton. I can also enlist the aid of the sheriff."

Partridge bristled. "I'm going with you."

"No. You must stay here, Lye. Bury those men and keep a watch. Protect Diandra. And if my partner shows up . . . tell him where to find me."

Diandra was staring at him. "Doc, I pray that Raider is alive."

"So do I," Doc replied glumly. "So do I."

CHAPTER TWELVE

The Gypsy woman's painted demon was hovering over Raider when he opened his black eyes. He cried out and tried to sit up. A pair of strong hands pushed him down. He felt warmth around him and realized that he was stark naked beneath fur blankets. When his eyes focused, he peered up into the painted face. The strong hand gripped the pendant around Raider's neck. An Indian was wearing Raider's old Stetson.

"Red Claw!"

The Arapaho brave smiled broadly at Raider.

"I musta fell into your private lake. Hell, boy, don't you ever get tired of savin' my worthless bacon?"

Raider glanced around the makeshift dwelling. It seemed logical that a renegade who didn't want to be found would take to the highest peak he could find. Red Claw reached behind his back for a bowl that he lifted to Raider's cracked lips. Raider drank a thick, salty-tasting liquid.

"This supposed to bring me around?"

If Red Claw understood the white man's tongue, he wasn't letting on. Instead, he clapped his hands and looked back over his shoulder. Two women appeared in the door of the crude wigwam. They had to be his squaws. Red Claw gestured and both of them dropped the furs that had been draped over their shoulders. Raider gawked at their nakedness.

Red Claw grunted and pulled back the fur covers. Raider's cock caught the squaws' attention.

He grinned nervously and clutched the covers to his chest. "I ain't the shy type, Red Claw, but I can't share your squaws."

Red Claw slapped his thighs. He was wearing Raider's clothes. He wanted to trade the squaws for the shirt and pants.

"Hell, you saved me, I reckon you can keep the pants. I got to wear something, though. Pants? You got pants?"

After a moment, Red Claw understood what he wanted. He left the wigwam and came back a few minutes later with a pair of buckskin pants. Raider slipped them on under the covers. When his legs and hips were covered, he tried to stand up. His muscles were weak, but he didn't ache as much as he had expected. Red Claw's potion must have helped some.

"I got to get out of here, boy. Understand? Me go."

Raider used the little sign language that he knew.

"Me. Go. Derby hat. Man with hat. Yeah, you're catching on."

They went outside. Red Claw's camp was sitting on the edge of the treeline above the mountain lake. Raider peered toward the blue and orange horizon to the east. He figured the sun would be up within the hour.

"I gotta get to Doc, Red Claw. If he's still alive."

Raider wondered if the cave-in had taken his partner's life. He peered into the forests. He sure as hell didn't know where he was, but he reckoned the quickest way back to the mine would be through the trees. He gestured to Red Claw, who seemed to understand him.

"You gonna take me out, boy? Me? Down? Yeah, that's the way. You got horses?"

Red Claw didn't have any mounts. Raider knew how he got around everywhere—he ran. An Indian could run for miles and never seemed to tire. Raider wondered if he could keep up with him.

"Where's my boots?"

They were on Red Claw's feet. Raider shook his head. He couldn't take them back, not after Red Claw had pulled him out of the lake. He saw a pair of moccasins lying next to the fire.

"I guess they're gonna have to do."

When his feet were covered, Raider wrapped a piece of cloth around his head. "Come on, boy. Let's move."

They ran through the trees until the ground began to slope downward. The trail was tougher then, but they made good time on the downhill grade. A sweat broke out on Raider's body, chasing most of the soreness from his muscles. At the bottom of the mountain Raider stopped, huffing and puffing.

"I gotta lay off the fatback." He looked up. "Where the hell are we?"

Red Claw started to run through the forest ahead of him. The ground leveled off onto the plain. Raider came out of the trees and glanced back to the north. Red Claw had brought him out on the wrong side of the mountain.

"Hell, now it's gonna take me a whole day to walk back to the mine."

But Red Claw didn't seem to understand him. The Arapaho brave gazed toward the south. Suddenly he plucked an arrow out of the quiver on his back and strung his pinewood bow.

"What the hell are you on to, Red Claw?"

Raider's black eyes peered southward. Dust stirred on the horizon. A rider was coming hell bent. Raider picked out the pearl gray derby when the horse was still a half mile away.

"No need for the bow, old buddy. Looks like a friend."

Doc reigned the chestnut mare that he had taken from the corral at the mining operation.

"My God, am I looking at a ghost?"

"There's no such thing as ghosts, Doc. You want to hear how I tried to bring down that balloon?"

Doc jumped off the horse and pointed to the blue sky ahead of them. "I see you weren't successful."

The dark orb floated over the peaks to the north. They could barely see it as it sailed toward the Wyoming border. Raider spun toward his partner.

"Let's get it, Doc!"

Doc shook his head. "He's got a twenty-mile-an-hour wind current pushing him north. We'd never catch him on horses."

Raider slapped his thigh. "Hell, Doc, he's got to come down sometime."

"We're helpless down here," Doc replied. "Of course . . ."

Raider regarded his partner with narrowed eyes. Doc wasn't telling him everything. When Doc left something unsaid, that meant there might be a way to figure something that was impossible."

"What is it, Doc?"

"Never mind, Raider, it would never work."

Raider grabbed the lapels of Doc's coat. "We ain't got forever on this thing, Doc. Now if you got somethin' cookin' up there in your noggin', you let it fly."

"Raider, I don't think we're prepared to take this kind of risk."

"Try me."

Doc brushed Raider's hands away. "Thank you."

"Come on, Doc. I know you're holding out on me."

Doc noticed Red Claw for the first time. "My word, where did our old friend come from?"

"He's been fishin' again."

"What?"

"I'll explain later, Doc. After you tell me what you're thinkin'."

Doc sighed. "Raider, I can see that you're not going to let this go, so I suppose I should tell you. There's a second balloon at the old Barlow place."

"How'd you find out about that?"

"After the tunnel collapsed, I headed back to the house. I found Delp and his men dead. The girl and young Partridge are still alive."

Raider grunted. "Ole Delp was a pretty good boy. Did you tell Lye about his pappy?"

Doc nodded. "There was no way to get through the rock wall that had fallen down, so I grabbed a horse and rode through the night to Horton. I got off a wire to the home office and asked the sheriff to accompany me to Partridge's lair."

"And they had already cleared out?"

"The balloon was rising as we rode over the ridge. The wind had shifted perfectly for them."

Raider glanced back toward the dot in the sky. "What about Wages, the science man?"

"He went with Partridge. They just wanted to clear out with what silver they had. I tell you, Partridge is completely mad."

"You always said that a madman leaves a wide trail."

Doc shook his head. "It doesn't matter when the madman can fly. Our only chance to catch him would be to fly after him."

Raider's eyes narrowed. "You say there's an extra balloon?"

"Correct. But it's not of the same design. It's an old hydrogen balloon."

"What were they doin' with two?"

"I suppose Partridge procured it before Wages designed the hot air device," Doc replied.

"You know how to work it?"

"I suppose I could. There's only one drawback, however. In the hot air balloon, Partridge can adjust the height by raising or lowering the flame. In the gas balloon, once we go up, we can only come down once."

Raider frowned. "Why's that?"

"We would have to let out the gas in order to descend."

"Didn't you say somethin' about balance?"

"Ballast," Doc replied. "I suppose we could work out something. Although I have my doubts about the hydrogen balloon. They can be very dangerous. A spark can set off a disastrous explosion."

Raider laughed. "Hell, it can't be that bad. At least you can't fire up one of them stink logs while we're flyin'. Flyin'. Son of a bitch."

Doc glanced at Red Claw. "We can ride double on my mount, but I'm afraid your friend here can't go."

"We left those mounts at the base of the mountain last night," Raider replied. "We can't be that far away."

Doc leapt into the saddle. "I'll get them."

Raider looked again toward the dot in the sky. "You get me to Partridge, Doc. I'll find a way to bring him down. And hurry, Doc. Hurry."

• • •

Raider jumped back when Doc turned the valve on the huge iron tank in Lymon Partridge's barn. A canvas hose ran from the tank to the limp bag that was sprawled all over the barnyard. Doc had spent two hours rigging the damned thing. As the bag started to expand, Red Claw howled a whooping war cry. Raider was starting to have second thoughts about flying.

Doc was very pleased with himself. "It won't be long now. Look at it. I'm going to use all the hydrogen so we'll be assured of getting off the ground."

"Yeah" was Raider's curt reply.

The balloon rose up into the sky. Raider had driven the stakes for the sky craft's tethers. He had argued with Doc about fixing the stakes before the balloon was filled. As the basket came up off the ground, Raider held his breath, wondering if the stakes would hold now. Doc hadn't underestimated the power of the lighter-than-air gas.

Raider was sweating. "Shit, Doc."

"Don't worry," Doc rejoined. "I'm just as scared as you. But as you can see, I've succeeded in raising the balloon. Only our mettle or lack of it stands in the way."

"What about the ballast thing?"

Doc raised his hand. "That I've solved. You see the sandbags around the edge? When we decide to land, I simply let out enough gas to allow our descent. Then we throw off the sand-bags when we want to rise again."

"So we'll be able to come back the same way?"

Doc shrugged. "Hopefully."

"Doc, if there's any burrs under this saddle, you better tell me now."

"We've taken worse risks. Are you game?"

Raider's black eyes were fretful. "I guess it's the only way to catch old Partridge before he gets clean away."

"I guess so."

"Hell, Doc, let's go get him."

Raider was the first one to climb over the side of the basket into the craft. Doc came behind him, shaking the lines that held the balloon to the earth. Raider took a second to find his legs. It was a lot like being on a boat, he thought.

"I'm going to cut the ropes," Doc said.

"What about if we land? How will we tie this thing down?"

Doc pointed to the lines coiled in the bottom of the basket. There were also a bottle of water and a jug of corn whiskey. Raider immediately took a swig of the mash. It burned going down, and it hit his nervous stomach like a rock.

"Cut her, Doc."

As Doc extended a sharp blade toward the rope, they felt the basket tilting. Raider looked over to see Red Claw climbing into the compartment. He had his bow strapped over his back, and he was still wearing his war paint. Doc glared at the tall Indian.

"I'm afraid he can't come along."

The Arapaho warrior was glaring back at Doc. Raider shrugged. "Sure, Doc. You want to tell him he ain't invited?"

"You do it, Raider."

"Nooo, uh-huh. This boy saved my life, Doc. Twice. Hell, if he wants to come along, I can't deny him."

Red Claw's savage face broke into a smile. He waved his hands upward, toward the sky. He had probably seen the other balloon come over the mountain many times. Now he wanted to be with the spirits in the blue expanse.

Doc gave in. "An unexpected crew member. I suppose he'll provide extra weight. Hold tight, Raider. Here goes."

Doc sawed through the ropes that held the balloon down. The basket wobbled as they soared off the earth. Doc hadn't expected such a quick ascent. Red Claw's weight was no burden. The clouds were drawing nearer. Had he used too much hydrogen?

Raider gaped toward the earth below. The colors had never seemed so well defined on the ground. The yellow plain met the green mountain forests along the banks of a sparkling river. As the wind pushed them north, he spied the Medicine Bow mining operation in the distance. An eagle soared into his sight line, casting a predator's sharp eye at the men in the sky.

Red Claw whooped and pointed toward the mountain. He wasn't afraid at all. He could see his camp next to the small lake.

"We may be going too high," Doc said. "The wind is getting stronger."

"Good," Raider replied. "We'll catch up to Partridge that much faster."

Doc looked nervous. "Yes, I suppose so."

Raider glared at his partner. "What's wrong with you all of a sudden? Hell, look at me and Red Claw. We're having a good time."

"I hope we aren't going too high."

"Are we in trouble, Doc?"

"I just don't know, Raider. I just don't know."

Raider stared out toward the clouds. "Don't worry, Doc. You just get us there. I'll find a way to do the rest."

The balloon sailed on in the quiet heavens, heading toward Wyoming at a steady clip.

CHAPTER THIRTEEN

"Yellowstone, Doc!"

They had been flying over Wyoming for two days, heading due north. Doc looked over the edge of the basket at the rough terrain below them. Steam rose out of the ground in a field of hot sulphur springs and geysers. Beyond the field, over a stretch of scraggled forest, lay the white peaks of the Rockies. Doc pulled his coat collar up around his neck. He was tired and cold and hungry. And there had been no sign of the other balloon.

"Yellowstone will be a good place to give it up," Doc said.

Raider clenched his teeth. "I hate givin' up. Hell, we don't never give up."

Doc looked up at the balloon. "We're losing altitude. We have been since last night. I think there's a slow leak above, on top."

Raider sat down again, leaning against the basket. "Hell, I reckon we might as well give up. Seein' as how we're fallin' and all."

"There will be park rangers here," Doc said. "A few years ago this area became a national park."

"Rangers. Whoopee."

Red Claw, who stood next to Doc, let out a screeching war cry. He pointed at the ground and grabbed Doc's shoulder. Doc strained to see what had caught the Arapaho's attention. If only he had his telescope.

Raider stood up. "What's ailin' him?"

"He sees something."

A brisk, icy wind pushed them toward the edge of the forest. Red Claw kept howling and pointing. His keen eyes were more adept at picking out a foreign object against the dark green hues of the woodland. Raider saw it before Doc. A half sphere rising above the treeline.

"He's got it tied up, Doc. But it won't be long before he sees us."

Doc put his hand on a valve that allowed the hydrogen to escape from the balloon. "Our only chance is to come down right on top of him."

"You got your Diamondback?"

Doc nodded.

Raider held out his hand. "Give it to me."

Without protest, Doc handed over the .38. Raider looked at the gun and shook his head. "I wish we had a little more firepower than this."

He kept his eyes trained on the other balloon. The wind had picked up, moving them closer at a steady speed. Doc estimated the velocity, trying to do the mathematics in his head. If the balloon was going so fast and it fell at such a rate . . . He just didn't know.

"Better turn that valve, Doc. He's seen us."

They were close enough for Raider to see the three tiny figures, hopping around the campsite like Texas June bugs. Red Claw howled again and lifted his hands to the sky. Maybe he had some score to settle with Partridge, Raider thought. A hissing sound startled Raider. Doc had opened the valve.

The basket dipped quickly. Doc turned the valve back and slowed the descent a little. But the ground still seemed to be coming up quickly. Raider could see Partridge and his men ahead of them.

"We're going to land a couple of hundred yards away," Doc said. "Look, he's heating up. If they get off the ground, we'll never catch them before they get up into Canada."

Red Claw grabbed Raider's shoulder. His face had slackened. He looked worried, Raider thought. He was staring at the campsite. Raider glanced up, but the close proximity of the ground was the only thing that caught his attention. Doc had turned off the valve, and the balloon seemed to be hovering about twenty feet above the rocky terrain.

Raider scowled at Doc. "How the hell we supposed to get down from here?"

Doc tossed a rope over the side of the basket. "I'll go first."

As Doc shinnied down the line, Raider turned back toward Partridge's campsite. The other balloon was still tied down. Raider wondered why no one had fired a shot at them. Red Claw cried out and went over the side of the basket without a rope.

"What the hell?"

Raider saw the smoke and the red sparkling of black powder. A whistling noise filled the air. Something was flying straight toward the balloon. He swung over the edge and started down the dangling line. A fireball exploded above him, and he fell the last ten feet to the earth. Doc and Red Claw grabbed his shoulders and pulled him away from the burning wreckage.

Raider scrambled to his feet. "What the hell was that, Doc?"

"One of Wages's little miracles."

"What?"

"A rocket, Raider. As in 'the rocket's red glare.'"

"'The bombs burstin' in air.' I know the song, Doc, only I don't see no flag anywhere."

Doc lit up a cigar. "You're lucky the damned thing didn't fall on top of you. If that fire had—"

Red Claw cried out from a slight rise above them. He gestured for Doc and Raider to join him. They hurried up the incline toward the adventurous brave. He pointed at Partridge's balloon. The rocket had brought them down a half mile away from the campsite.

"They think we're dead," Doc said. "If we could sneak around into the forest, perhaps we could come up behind them and—"

"Too late now, Doc."

The balloon came up off the ground. Partridge wasn't taking any chances. He was going to run, in case the Pinkertons had reinforcements in the area. Doc would have settled for a couple of good rifles.

"Goodbye to Mr. Partridge."

Raider looked at Red Claw. "Maybe not. Give me that bow, you wild Injun. Yeah, I want it."

Red Claw slipped the pinewood bow off his back. Raider tried it for pull. Then he took an arrow from the quiver and looked at Doc.

"Give me that handkerchief you got in your pocket. Come on, Weatherbee, don't just stand there gawkin'. Hand it over."

Doc gave him the handkerchief. "What are you going to try, Raider?"

"Give me that flask and your sulphur matches."

"Raider, I don't see how you can hope to—"

"Shut up, Doc, and do it!"

Doc surrendered the flask and matches. Raider wrapped the handkerchief around the end of the arrow, leaving the stone arrowhead uncovered. Then he soaked the handkerchief with the contents of the flask.

"That's my best brandy!"

Raider peered back toward the rising balloon. "Don't worry, Doc, it ain't goin' to be wasted."

"What are you going to do, Raider?"

"I'm gonna fire a little rocket of my own, Doc." He turned to Red Claw. "You ready to run, buddy?"

Red Claw laughed and flapped his arms like a bird. Raider shook his head and started for the balloon at a full run. Red Claw took off behind him. Doc watched as they ate up the ground, closing the distance on the ballon, both of them howling like a couple of banshees.

Bursts of gunfire erupted from the basket of the balloon. The basket had reached tree level. It wasn't taking off as fast as Partridge had hoped. Doc started walking toward the campsite, keeping his eye on his partner.

Raider ran in zigzag patterns, making it hard for the rifles above to reach him. When he was directly under the balloon, he stopped and struck a sulphur match. He torched the end of the fire arrow and notched it in the pinewood bow. The stream of flame arched skyward like a comet, landing in the gray cloth of the balloon. Raider jumped up and down. The barking rifle urged him back toward Doc. Red Claw was right in his tracks.

Doc gazed up in disbelief at the flames on Partridge's balloon. It wouldn't explode like the hydrogen craft. The basket swung out over the forest, urged northward by the wind. A body flew over the side, crashing into the branches below.

"He threw somebody out!" Raider cried. "I'll bet it was Wages."

"It doesn't matter. At the rate those flames are eating his balloon, he won't get far. He'll have to come down in the woods."

Raider handed the pinewood bow to Red Claw. The brave laughed and clapped Raider on the back. Then he started off for the woods on his own. Raider wondered if they had seen the last of him.

"Dang me, Doc, if somethin' ain't weird about him showin' up like that. Maybe somethin' is watchin' over me."

Doc was still peering at the forest. The balloon was beginning to sink from the sky, a trail of smoke marking its demise. "We have two choices, Raider. We can go after the authorities, or we can pursue Partridge on our own."

"Hell, I think we ought to at least take a look, Doc. Maybe he'll crash that thing. What if they ain't even alive?"

"You keep the Diamondback, Raider."

"Right here in my belt. Or whatever you call these buckskin things."

They walked along the edge of the woodland until they found something that resembled a trail. Doc thought Raider rather enjoyed running around half naked like an Indian. The big man from Arkansas preceded him, disappearing between the branches of juniper. Doc plodded along until the whooping cry resounded through the trees.

The balloon had come down about a mile inside the forest, landing between two ponderosa pines. A huge hole had been opened by Raider's fire arrow, but the entire balloon hadn't burned.

Raider pointed up at the lines that hung from the basket.

"They let themselves down," Raider said. "Here are the tracks, two sets going in different directions. He musta throwed out Wages. Here's that midget's footprints. Little one's headin' back into the trees. Partridge is headin' out."

Doc looked up at the balloon basket. "One of us should go up to see if they left any firearms behind."

Raider grabbed the rope and climbed to the basket. He rummaged around and came up with an old Navy Colt. It was a percussion loader with only two chambers packed. When he came back down, he gave Doc the Diamondback.

Doc looked at the Navy Colt. "Will that be enough for you?"

"Hell, if I don't get him, you will."

"Raider, I've been thinking. We should split up. You go after the little man and I'll chase Partridge."

Raider squinted at his partner. "You want me to go after that midget?"

"I have two reasons. First, both of them have to be brought to justice. Second, I want to bring Partridge back alive. I think his son has the right to see him."

Raider bristled. "Hell, after all I done you don't trust me to keep my trigger finger quiet! I mean, I brung down that balloon after you give up. I find this in the trees and you want me to go after a pint-sized peckerwood."

"We're wasting time, Raider."

'Yeah."

"Do you want the Diamondback?"

Raider grunted. "For a midget? Hell, Doc, why don't you scare us up a Gatlin' gun? Or a Stokes mortar!"

Doc ignored him and peered in the direction where Partridge had run. "If I recall our aerial view, there's a bed of hot springs and geysers on the eastern edge of this forest."

"And I got to go back into the trees."

Doc smiled. "At least you're dressed for the occasion."

"Hell, I guess it makes sense for you to chase ole Partridge. He's damned smart, but I suppose you're smarter."

"Thank you, Raider. I'll take that as a compliment."

Raider started off through the trees. "No compliment intended. I just see it that way."

"Be careful."

'Oh yeah," Raider called back. "I'm only chasin' somebody that's half as big as me. I'll be careful, all right!"

Doc looked down at Partridge's footprints and started to follow them through the trees.

CHAPTER FOURTEEN

Raider was pretty damned tired of fighting the terrain. The little man's trail had gone into a rough section of rocks and brush. Naturally it was easier for the dwarf to scoot around between the boulders and the greasewood. Yellowstone was spooky wilderness. He might never find him.

Raider leaned back against a rock, wiping his brow. It was high noon. The sun had burned away all of the morning coolness. He'd have to find a drink of water in a hurry. His mouth was cotton-spitting dry.

He continued on, northwest. When he had been in the balloon, he had gazed toward the open place between the forest and the mountain. The little man would have a long way to go before he reached the Rockies. Raider knew he was close by. Those stumpy legs wouldn't hold up all day.

Raider picked up the trail again, making his way until he heard a slight trickling of water. He found a spring pool between two rocks. The water was warm and tasted of sulphur. He wet his lips and washed his face. When a rock tumbled down into the spring, Raider picked up the Navy Colt and stepped backward.

"There you are, you little ole feller."

The dwarf stood on the rocks above the hot spring. His hands were behind his back. Raider thumbed the hammer of the Navy Colt.

"Drop whatever it is that you're holdin' behind your back, shorty!"

"My name is Brutus."

His manner was gentle and childlike. Raider smiled. He didn't know if he could bring himself to shoot the frog-faced little critter.

"Brutus, why don't you hop on down here and let me take you on back to Denver. You'll get a fair trial. Hell, if you ain't killed nobody, you might even get off with a couple of years."

The little man brought out the sawed-off from behind his back. He thumbed both hammers and pointed the double barrels at Raider. "I'm going free, cowboy."

"Don't force me to use this pistol, Brutus. I don't want to kill you."

Brutus looked down the stunted barrel. "Turn around, Pinkerton. Turn around and go, or I'll blast you straight to hell."

Raider pulled the trigger of the Colt. The percussion cap fizzled. He tried the second chamber, which was also a dud. He peered down the bore of the sawed-off.

"I've got you now, Pinkerton." The little devil was smiling. "I'm a big man now. Say it. Say, 'Brutus is a big man.'"

"Aw, kiss my ass, you little pissant."

Brutus looked like he was about to cry. "You're going to die. I gave you a chance, but now you're going to die."

Raider dived for the ground, expecting to hear the dual eruption of the shotgun barrels. When the scattergun didn't go off, he rolled over to look at Brutus. The dwarf was teetering on the rocks. He slipped forward and fell face-first into the hot spring. Raider stood up and slowly approached the body. An Arapaho arrow was lodged between the tiny shoulder blades.

"Damn you, Red Claw! How many lives do I have to owe you, you damned fool Injun!"

Red Claw's reply came in the form of haughty laughter that rang through the dense, rocky wasteland.

Doc had expected an ambush. The unknown force of scientific knowledge lashing out at him from Partridge's evil mind.

With his .38 Diamondback in hand, he followed the signs that Raider had trained him to see—a broken branch, a stepped-on lichen, the mark of a boot heel on stone. As the forest sloped downward, Doc could smell the acrid stench of the sulphur springs. He paused, waiting for Partridge to drop out of a tree.

But nothing came. Doc kept on, trudging onto the steaming plain of geysers and hot springs. He scanned the plateau, looking for any sign of Partridge. A vague figure moved through the steam ahead of him. He was dragging a leg that had been damaged in the crash. Blood marked the hard surface of the igneous rock.

"Partridge! Give up."

When the echo of Doc's voice reached him, Partridge spun around and looked back through the steam. Doc started toward him, the Diamondback at his side. Partridge began to limp away from him, fleeing like a wounded bear.

Doc strode between the steaming pools of water, calling after his adversary. "You can't escape, Partridge. Why don't you come back like a man? Take your medicine. It would make your son proud of you."

Partridge replied with a rifle that he took from his long coat. A slug whizzed by Doc's head. Doc hit the ground, hiding in the billows of vapor. The rifle lever chortled again.

"If you kill me, someone else will come after you, Partridge. My partner will find you. He won't be as merciful as I—"

A geyser burst up next to Doc, flying high into the air with a forceful jet of water. Hot liquid drenched Doc from head to foot. He held his pistol underneath his body, trying to keep it from getting wet. He didn't want to kill Lymon Partridge, but he wanted to be ready if Partridge refused to give him a choice.

Partridge's footsteps were audible because he had to drag the bad leg. Doc marked him in the steam, coming closer with the rifle in hand. When he was in front of him, Doc raised up with the Diamondback.

"Far enough, sir. Drop the rifle and turn back toward me."

Partridge was not quick enough to get the drop on him. He had to let go of the rifle and raise his hands. Doc forced him to back away from the weapon.

"I'm sorry that it had to come to this," Doc said as he picked up the rifle. "You should have been happy to have your share.

Your son admitted that it was indeed Bixley who found the claim."

Partridge's face resembled the Satan mask in the steam. Doc wondered where all the hatred had come from. He stepped back cautiously. A madman was often capable of great feats of strength.

"All of them are telling you lies, Weatherbee!"

"Why didn't you kill your son, Partridge?"

The mad eyes registered pain. "What are you talking about, Pinkerton?"

"When you made your last run on the mine, you had Short go below and kill the other men. Yet he didn't kill Lye or Diandra. You ordered him to tie them up. Didn't you?"

"I don't . . . I don't remember."

"Do you love your son, Partridge? Is that why you wouldn't let Short kill him? Answer me!"

Partridge clutched his head in his hands. "The pain! Make it stop! Make it stop hurting!"

He spun away from Doc and started running pell-mell through the fields of geysers. Doc had to chase him, stepping between the pools of sulphuric heat. He was taken aback that Partridge could run so fast with the game leg. Another insane surprise.

Doc fired a warning shot into the air. "No farther, Partridge!"

But he didn't stop. He kept stumbling forward, finally tripping on a hole in the earth and falling flat on his face. He was played out. As Doc walked toward the pitiful figure, he could hear him mumbling to himself.

"There's a worm in my brain that makes me do these things. There's a little round worm . . ."

Before Doc could reach him, he felt a trembling in the ground. Partridge's body quivered violently. He screamed out as the water gushed from the bowels of the earth. The geyser lifted his body high into the air, buffeting him in a circular motion at the top of the shooting column of water. When the geyser subsided, Partridge fell fifty feet to the hard stone.

The body just lay there motionless. Doc crept up on him, half expecting the geyser to erupt again. He grabbed the tail of Partridge's coat, pulling him off the gurgling hole. The cracked skull rolled to one side. Doc peered into the blood-gray cavity. Lodged in the brain, between the ruts, was a vile, black substance. A demon, Doc thought. The demon, whatever it might be, that had climbed into Lymon Partridge's brain to make him hurt everyone who had loved him. Doc looked away from the mess.

He stood up and gazed out over the field. Taking hold of the dead man's feet, he started to drag him away from the steaming pits of Hell. It had been a fitting place for Satan to die.

The man in uniform approached Doc on horseback. His creases were all in place, and he sported a round, wide-brimmed leather hat. He looked down at the body Doc had been dragging. A pistol appeared in his gloved hand.

"You'll raise your hands at once, sir."

Doc obeyed him. "No need for the gun. I have done nothing wrong."

The man in uniform raised an eyebrow. "I heard shots and came to investigate. I find you dragging a dead man down the trail. Is it not fair to assume that you have killed him?"

"If you will allow me to reach into my coat pocket, I can prove that I am an operative of the Pinkerton National Detective Agency. I have been in pursuit of this man and indeed, have finally apprehended him. If you are a ranger, sir, I would—"

"Be slow with your hands, sir."

Doc convinced him that he was not a murderer. The ranger stepped off the black gelding to look at the body. Doc told him the whole story, including the way Partridge had died.

The ranger tipped back his hat. "Truly a remarkable tale. And you say that another man is lying dead in those woods?"

"Possibly two more, if Raider is up to his usual tricks."

The ranger's eyes narrowed. "Raider?"

"My partner. I sent him after the dwarf."

"This is sounding more and more farfetched, sir."

Doc nodded. "I understand. But if you'll come with me . . ."

"What do you want to do with this unfortunate soul?"

Doc looked down at Partridge. "We'll take him. If we leave him, he'll probably fall victim to scavengers. Shall we tie him onto your horse?"

When the body was hanging over the saddle, Doc and the ranger started toward the forest. "We should probably keep an eye peeled for Red Claw."

The ranger looked dubious. "The Arapaho?"

"Yes, he was the Indian I told you about. He's still on the loose hereabouts. Although he has been friendly so far."

His new friend was shaking his head. "Can't be so, sir. Red Claw was killed about five years back. He's buried in the mountains above Medicine Bow."

Doc was not going to argue. "If you say so, sir."

As they approached the trees, Raider came out with the dwarf flung over his shoulders. The ranger stopped and pulled his pistol. Raider kept coming at them.

"No need for alarm," Doc said. "That's only my partner."

"He's a rough-looking sort."

"Even rougher in disposition," Doc replied.

Raider came up next to them and dropped the body at Doc's feet. "I went after him, just like you said. Who's the soldier boy?"

"I am Malcolm Stone, corporal U.S. Army, on special assignment to this region. I have the responsibility of patroling this park."

"How come you ain't wearin' a blue suit?"

The ranger snapped to attention. "A special assignment warrants a special uniform."

"Hey, don't take no offense. That brown looks a hell of a lot better than the blue." He saw Partridge's corpse. "You had some luck too, huh, Doc? You have to shoot him?"

Doc shook his head. "He was thrown in the air by the force of a geyser. When he hit the ground, his skull cracked open."

Raider ran a hand over his own skull. "Tough way to go. You gonna lower that pistol, soldier boy?"

"I'm not sure," the ranger replied. "I don't know quite what to think. All of these bodies. And I've no way to corroborate your story."

Raider laughed. "Hell, partner, you just walk back up there in them woods. 'Bout a mile back you'll find the rest of that balloon. And ole Wages, the brain man, is somewhere in those trees. Partridge tried to give him wings, but he just couldn't fly."

The ranger rolled the body of Lymon Partridge out of the saddle. "I'm going to take a look for myself. I suggest you gentlemen stay right here."

Raider called to him as he rode toward the woods. "Don't worry, soldier man, we ain't goin' nowhere."

Doc pulled out an Old Virginia cheroot. "Do you still have my matches, Raider?"

"I lost 'em in the woods."

"No matter."

Doc used a small magnifying glass to ignite a handful of dried brush. He torched the end of the cigar. Raider made coughing noises, but Doc enjoyed a good smoke. They were quiet for a while, watching the forest.

"What do we do now?" Raider asked finally.

"Wait for the ranger."

Raider fanned away the smoke. "I mean after the soldier comes back."

Doc yawned. "Oh, I don't know. I suppose our friend there has a station nearby. If we can find a telegraph office, we can send a message to the main office and then procure some horses."

Raider looked at the bodies. "We takin' them along?"

"Only Partridge."

"Aw, Doc, I—"

"Lye Partridge will see his father one more time."

Raider didn't feel like arguing. He stayed downwind of the smoke, keeping his eyes on the trees. The ranger's pistol fired a signal that echoed over the rolling landscape. No doubt, thought Doc, he had found the deceased figure of Elton Wages where he had tumbled to his destiny from the sky. As they ran to meet the ranger, Doc was sorry that he would never get to meet the man who had masterminded the haunting silver theft at Medicine Bow.

CHAPTER FIFTEEN

In a patch of forest just below the Medicine Bow mining operation, Lymon Partridge was buried next to Tiny Delp and the other men who had died at the hand of Partridge and his henchmen. Lye Partridge showed little emotion as they lowered the pine box into the hole. It had taken them two weeks to get the body back to Medicine Bow.

When the coffin was resting in the grave, Lye glanced up at Doc. "Mr. Weatherbee, would you say a few words?"

Doc was holding his pearl gray derby against his chest. "The world takes certain men before their time. Who knows why? Good night, sweet prince, a flight of angels sing thee to thy rest. From *Hamlet*. Your father, like the young Dane, was tortured by his demons. He is at peace now."

A tear rolled down Lye's cheek. "Thank you, Mr. Weatherbee."

Doc remembered the words of Homer: "Few sons are like their fathers; some are better, most are worse." Lye was holding up well. Doc wondered if the young man blamed himself for his father's degeneration.

Diandra stepped up next to Doc and slid her arm in his. "Thank you again for bringing him back."

"Diandra, would you say a couple of kind words to Raider? He's been rather glum since Lye's arrival. I think he rather fancied you."

She nodded and moved over next to the big man from Arkansas.

Raider shifted nervously in his new boots. "We didn't mean to kill him, Diandra. It just sort of—"

"Shh. It's all right. Lye's daddy was never the same after the war. He came back bitter. Lye left home because he thought his father hated him. He never knew there was something wrong in his head."

Lye Partridge started to shovel dirt into the grave.

Diandra put her hand on Raider's forearm. "Raider, if Lye hadn't come back . . ." She blushed. "Well, I think things could have been different. You are a fine figure of a man and—"

"Keep goin', honey. I like what you're sayin'."

Diandra was staring behind him. Raider turned around and looked down toward the trail. Rattling harnesses cut the still air of Sunday morning. A buckboard was passing the miner's quarters. Hobert Bixley swayed in the wooden seat.

"Father!" Diandra cried.

She ran to meet him. Bixley scolded his daughter for not telling him she was coming to Medicine Bow. She was so tearful, however, that he couldn't stay angry with her. Diandra led him to the grave site, trying to explain what had happened. Bixley could not follow the story.

Bixley turned to Doc and Raider. "Figured I come up here and see how y'all have been spending my money, Weatherbee. Here I find you buryin' a man that's been dead for months. Have you done anything toward solving the problems of this mine?"

Lye Partridge stepped away from his father's grave. "They've done everything to solve your problems, sir."

"Lye! When did you get here?"

Doc took hold of Bixley's arm. "Sir, if you will retire with us to the house, we will fill you in on everything."

Doc elaborated on the details of the case, citing everything from his case report. Bixley sipped brandy, trying to keep the pieces together. Finally it sunk in, and he leaned back with a dour look on his face.

"My own partner, a thief," he said sadly. "I trusted that man with my life so many times. I can't believe what you are saying."

Doc leaned in toward Bixley. "I didn't want to tell your daughter or Lye, but I discovered something about your former partner. When he was killed, he sustained an injury that opened up his skull. I saw a black substance inside his head. Now, I know very little of these things. They are called tumors. I stopped at Fort Laramie and spoke to the Army surgeon. He examined the tumor and did have knowledge of other cases where madness had set in slowly, with the growth in the brain."

Bixley shook his head and drained his brandy snifter. "Are you saying that this . . . tumor may have been responsible for my partner's insanity?"

"I can only attest to what I saw. It's simply something for consideration. And it might help you to retain a fond memory of him. You must have been good friends at one time."

"The best of friends," Bixley replied.

Raider, who had left the room in the middle of Doc's story, strode into the dining room with a wooden box in his hands. He plunked it down at Bixley's feet. Bixley looked over at Doc with a helpless expression in his eyes.

"Your silver," Doc said. "There's more upstairs in the loft. Partridge spent some of it to finance his scheme, but we got back a great deal of it."

Bixley laughed. "And I was coming up here to scold you for not doing your job. Gentlemen, I commend you. A toast. But I can't toast you with an empty glass. Where's that daughter of mine?"

Diandra flowed into the room with a bottle of brandy on a tray. Her cheeks were a blushing red. Lye Partridge came in right behind her. He was smiling like a possum, Raider thought. Something was up.

Diandra filled her father's glass. "Daddy, Lye has something he wants to ask you."

Doc stood up. "Raider, perhaps we should retire to the back porch."

"Why not?"

Raider trailed Doc out of the house. He sat down on the back porch, gazing gloomily toward the mine.

Doc offered him the flask of brandy. "Looking for more spirits?"

Raider shook his head. "You know what ole Lye is gonna ask Diandra's pa, don't you?"

"Yes, he will no doubt ask for her hand in marriage."

"Hell, Doc, just once I'd like to end up with a girl like Diandra. She's special, you know what I mean? Like that Kathy girl of yours back in Denver. I never end up with a special girl."

Doc shifted nervously. "Speaking of Kathryn, she came to Bixley's office, asking after me. It seems my scheme, or rather, your scheme worked. She wants me to accompany her to Omaha if I can get back to Denver before the fifteenth. Would you like to come along?"

Raider sighed and shook his head. "Naw, I'm just feelin' sorry for myself. Maybe I'll ride on down to Denver with you, but I can wait there while you head east with your lady."

Doc sat up and listened to the wind. "Raider, do you hear that?"

"What?"

"I distinctly hear chimes!"

Raider leaned forward and listened. He remembered the sound from the Gypsy woman's camp. He also heard the thudding of hooves and the rattling of a rickety cart. She was making him hear it in her magic way.

"Doc, I reckon I'll just slip on down the back here. I'll see you in Denver."

"Very well. Do be careful."

As Raider hurried down toward his mount, he had to laugh at Doc's admonition. Careful wasn't for a man who had flown, fallen, and attacked the Devil. Careful wasn't for the man who was going to spend a week in the warm, dark arms of Medea Barnado.

EPILOGUE

Hard summer rain pelted Raider as he listed in the saddle of the roan gelding. He had been riding hard for three days, and he was still a two-day ride from Nampa, Idaho. A sheriff there was holding a prisoner who was wanted in Kansas for murdering somebody in the state government. The state department of justice figured it was cheaper to hire a Pinkerton for the extradition.

The roan plodded toward the darkening horizon. Night came on unmercifully, bringing with it continuing sheets of hard rain. Raider hid under the brim of his Stetson, watching the water roll off his slicker. He was thinking about things that he usually tried to avoid.

Brooding thoughts, like an angry grandmother. A man didn't have much. Nothing stayed with a man. Not even a rich man. And a man who rode wild-asses into the stormy wilderness didn't have a damned thing.

The roan collapsed underneath him. Raider rolled into the mud. He stood up and peered for a moment toward heaven. That's what he got for brooding. Now it was worse. He sat there for several hours in the darkness, waiting to see if the roan was finished. When the horse stood up on his own, Raider led him on in the storm.

A man didn't have a damned thing.

Raider's body straightened when he saw the light in the distance. It wasn't a sharp light, only a watery glow in the deluge. The roan was able to keep up when Raider broke into a run. It was a big dwelling that seemed too large for a trading post.

At the stoop, a black man appeared to take his horse, just like he had been expected for dinner. Raider stomped up the steps, calling back for the full treatment for his mount. The door of the house swung open before he could knock. A red-haired woman, missing several front teeth, smiled at Raider.

"Get on in here, cowboy. Whoo-wee, girls, looks like we got one man that's not afraid to come out on a stormy Saturday night."

She guided Raider into a fancy receiving parlor. Feathered ladies were sprawled about, tending their vanities. Raider wondered if he had died out on the plain and been taken to heaven by the storm. Maybe a bolt of lightning had struck him.

"What's the matter, cowboy?" the redhead asked.

"Pardon me, ma'am, but would you mind tellin' me where I am? I just rode in from south of here."

The redhead laughed. "Honey, you're just outside Boise. It's Saturday night, and you're in for a little fun."

Raider took off his Stetson. "Looks like Lady Luck finally turned my way."

"We ain't got no Lady Luck," replied the redhead, "but I'm available for a couple of hours."

"I don't mean to push my luck, but I've got a few pesos. Could you see fit to spot me a room for the night? And maybe a bath."

"Twenty-five dollars." She said it like she thought Raider would refuse.

"Here's a double eagle," he replied, flipping her the gold coin. "I'll give you the rest when I leave. Here's another buck for some whiskey and two bits for a plate of grub."

"I like your manners, cowboy. Don't forget, you can have your pick of my girls. It's a rainy night, so there's quite a selection."

Raider circled around the room, peering into pretty faces. He couldn't remember why he had felt so hateful before. There were plenty of things for a man who knew where to look. Of course, he had to be lucky once in a while.

He took the hand of a large-breasted woman with dark hair. "Come on, honey. I need somebody to wash my back."

A man could have a lot of things if he had enough silver in his pocket.

Raider led her up the stairs to the bathroom. As she bent over the tub to soak his back, her breasts brushed against the back of his head. Raider turned around, kissing her round nipples.

"Has it been a long time, cowboy?"

"Long enough."

"Who was she, your last girl? Tell me about her."

"Just a crazy Gypsy woman who tried to drive me loco."

He pulled her hand down beneath the water. "Why don't you soap my pecker, honey?"

She rolled his thick cock between her fingers. "Umm, you're doing just fine. I can see why you chose me. I'm a big girl."

Raider pushed her hand away. "Well, big girl, why don't you get naked and join me in this tub?"

She stepped back away from him, letting her flimsy peignoir fall to the floor. Her legs came over the edge of the tub. She sat down in the water, lowering her bushy wedge toward Raider's cock. Her fingers guided him into the warmth of her cunt. Even if a man didn't have much, Raider thought, what he had was enough. In fact, it was plenty.